Encounter...

Gail stared at the tall young man getting out of the car. It couldn't be Larry Stillman! But it was, and he paused at the gate to study her curiously.

"Well, hello there," he said at last. He swung open the gate and came into the patio. Uninvited, he dropped into a chair across from her.

"I'd forgotten how pretty you are, Gail."

"Had you?" Her voice stuck in her throat.

He nodded. "In fact," he admitted with a frankness she found bitterly humiliating, "I'm afraid I'd forgotten just what you looked like. But now that I've refreshed my memory, I intend to stick around for a while . . .

**PUT PLEASURE IN YOUR READING
Larger type makes the difference**
THIS EASY EYE Edition is set in large, clear type—at least 30 percent larger than usual. It is printed on scientifically tinted non-glare paper for better contrast and less eyestrain.

The Trusting Heart
Peggy Dern

VALENTINE BOOKS
NEW YORK

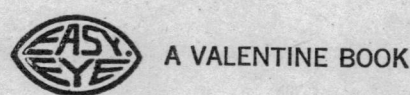 A VALENTINE BOOK

THE TRUSTING HEART

Copyright © 1961 by Arcadia House
All rights reserved
Printed in the U.S.A.

Valentine Books are published by
PRESTIGE BOOKS, INC., 18 EAST 41ST STREET
NEW YORK, N.Y. 10017

Chapter One

The huge bus sped through the small towns, the hammock land, the stands of tall pines, and Gail Harrison leaned close to the window, reveling in scenery that was new and strange to her.

This, she reminded herself, her heart beating faster, was Florida, Larry's Florida! Within another hour or two she would leave the bus at the end of the line: Grove City, Larry's town.

She couldn't think of anything except Larry. She would step directly from the bus into Larry's arms, and maybe by this time tomorrow, or the day after, she would be Larry's wife!

It was a word that brought a happy glow to her heart; a word she had never thought would be applied to her, with Aunt Louisa holding her a virtual prisoner. Oh, she shouldn't call herself a prisoner, she corrected her thought with swift loyalty. Aunt Louisa had needed her and had been good to her and she owed it to her aunt to do everything she could to repay the obligations she had incurred when she came to live with Aunt Louisa at the age of five.

"I was fond of your father, Frederick," Aunt Louisa was fond of saying. "But when he insisted on marrying a girl as far beneath him socially as Enid Dale, I disowned him. So you really have no right to impose on my kindness and generosity. I owe you absolutely nothing. It's you who are in my debt."

Gail had never been allowed to date; she always had to hurry straight home from school to wait on Aunt Louisa, whose health was so bad that she was practically a semi-invalid. Only two afternoons a week, when three of Aunt Louisa's elderly cronies came in to drink tea and play bridge and gossip, was Gail free for an hour. And it was during one of those hours that, quite by accident, she had met Larry Stillman.

Even now, months later, the memory brought a smile to her pretty mouth and a dreamy look to her brown-gold eyes. She had been walking along the bridle path that separated Aunt Louisa's property from that of the very wealthy Stillmans. And she had heard the gallop of hooves, and had just managed to scramble out of the way before a beautiful chestnut gelding ridden by a handsome young man, came bursting around a curve in the path. She had scrambled out of the way and had fallen beside the bridle path. The rider had hastily managed to stop his horse, to spring down beside her, to assure himself she was not hurt. At first he had been very angry with her for being on land posted against trespassing. And then when she had explained that she walked in the woods on the two afternoons she was free, because she could be away from the house only an hour, he had been curious. He had asked a lot of questions about herself, Aunt Louisa and the town that lay two miles away.

She had known, of course, who he was. The arrival of Larry Stillman, who had inherited the famous racing stables of his uncle and who was there to dispose of the property, had been discussed from one end of the county to the other. He was even more handsome and dashing than she had been led to expect by the gossip she had heard. And he seemed to find her interesting.

She had fallen headlong in love with him within minutes of that first meeting. And in subsequent meetings, those stolen hours when Aunt Louisa and her friends were happily playing bridge, Larry had said that he loved her too. She had been dazed and incredulous; but when he had held her close and hard in his arms and kissed her, she could no longer doubt him. She had wept stormily, because she knew she could never marry him. She owed Aunt Louisa too much; Aunt Louisa needed her too badly.

Larry had become fairly violent at that. He had insisted that "some day" they would be married. But Gail, knowing that "some day" could only mean after Aunt Louisa's death, had shuddered. And so Larry had held her close, kissed her tenderly and gone away, leaving her in heartbroken tears.

Then the most amazing, the most incredulous thing had happened to set her free to marry Larry! He had gone away in the spring, after the sale of the racing stables; and Gail had spent a heartsick, grieving summer until the afternoon the three old ladies arrived for their bridge game, so excited they could barely talk. For Miss Susie, the richest of the four, had discovered a personally conducted tour of Europe arranged by a travel agency specializing in elderly people and semi-invalids who yearned for a trip abroad but were fearful of risking the physical hazards. The tour would include nurses and attendants; there would always be a doctor within easy reach; and there was really, Miss Susie insisted eagerly, no difficulty whatever.

Gail listened, wide-eyed, to the chatter. Miss Susie had sold her two friends, Miss Letty and Miss Martha, on the trip; and they wanted Miss Louisa to go, too. It had been Dr. Barker who had given the four his complete approval of the trip, and Aunt Louisa had been as excited as Miss Susie when the time for departure approached.

Gail all but held her breath. Would she be taken, too? And then the night before the four were to leave, Aunt Louisa had looked up from her perusal of the agency's brochure and had watched Gail packing.

"There's just one thing that bothers me, Gail," she announced flatly. "That's what I'm going to do with you."

Gail straightened, her red-brown head lifted, her eyes wide.

"You don't want me to go with you, Aunt Louisa?" she asked.

Aunt Louisa scowled. "Go with me? Now that's a silly question. I shan't need you, so why should I add to the expense of the journey? Susie's nurse will accompany us to New York by plane. There the agency will take over, and we'll be properly looked after by trained nurses throughout the whole trip."

Gail said uneasily, "Then would you like me to just stay on here?"

Aunt Louisa's eyebrows went up.

"Here in this big house alone? Certainly not!" she said in her usual irascible tone. "I've put the house up for sale, and the real estate man is sure he can dispose of it immediately. So what to do with you I simply can't imagine. You don't have any training for a job. But then I've supported you all these years and you're twenty years old. It seems to me you're quite old enough to get a job and shift for yourself."

"Oh, I can, Aunt Lou. I can," Gail said eagerly. "You musn't worry about me."

"I didn't intend to," snapped Aunt Louisa. "After all, you're a big girl now, and surely I've done enough for you. I've put some money in this envelope. It should take care of you until you find some sort of job. And when that's gone, I'm afraid you'll be on your own."

"And it's high time I was, Aunt Lou, you've been very good to me."

Aunt Louisa sniffed. "Well, I'm glad you realize that. I've certainly tried. Now get on with the packing. And be sure you don't overlook anything I'm likely to need. Things will be very expensive in New York, and I imagine even more so abroad. Be sure you include all my medicines."

"Yes, Aunt Lou," said Gail above the joyous rioting of her heart.

The following day, she saw Aunt Louisa and her three friends board the plane that would take them to New York. Gail had stood at the edge of the airfield watching as the giant silver bird lifted into the sky and winged north.

Then she had gone straight to the telegraph office and sent Larry a wire announcing her imminent arrival. She had taken the five hundred dollars Aunt Louisa had given her, found out the price of a bus ticket to Grove City, put a twenty-dollar bill in reserve, and had recklessly and joyously squandered the rest on pretty clothes. Her trousseau packed away in a modestly priced suitcase, because there was no sense in spending any of her precious money for expensive luggage, she had climbed aboard the bus.

And now here she was, within an hour of Grove City and Larry's waiting arms. She went back to the lounge and freshened herself as much as its confines would permit. And when the bus slid into the station at Grove City, she was the first passenger to leave it.

She looked about her. Grove City was a small town, and the bus had not been crowded. There were two other buses loading, one for Tampa, the other for Miami. There were quite a few people milling around in the station, and Gail's anxious, eager eyes searched for Larry, her heart beating so hard she felt sure it must sound like a set of bongo drums.

Gradually, the Tampa and Miami buses loaded and pulled away. The crowd thinned, until there were not more than half a dozen people on the platform. And not one of them bore the slightest resemblance to Larry.

Her heart sank a little. Hadn't he received her telegram? Her last letter from him two weeks ago had been mailed from there.

A tall, sun-bronzed, black-haired man in his

late twenties, wearing slacks and a brilliantly patterned sports shirt, had been loitering near the entrance to the station. Now he turned away, hesitated, looked back scowlingly at Gail, standing beside her modest luggage, and turned away again. And then, as if he knew that he was doing something foolish, he came striding toward her, his brows drawn together in a dark scowl.

"Look, you can't possibly be Gail Harrison, can you?" he demanded.

"Oh," she looked up at him swiftly, "I am. But you're not Larry."

For a moment of utter astonishment the man stood quite still, his eyes taking her in from the top of her rumpled curls to the tips of her slippers.

"So you're Gail Harrison," he said at last, and there was a look of active dislike in his eyes that bewildered her. "Larry asked me to meet you. He's out of town."

Gail caught her breath on a small despairing moan.

"Oh, I suppose I should have wired him earlier, so he would have had time to answer," she began.

"That might have been an excellent idea," said the man curtly. "I'm Troy Benton, and I work for Larry. I'm to take you home with me, for my sister to look after until Larry comes back."

Gail said huskily, "I have some money. Maybe I could go to a hotel."

"How much money?" demanded Troy. Gail

stammered the amount that was left of the twenty she had put aside. "That would last you for about a day here. No, it's much better for you to come home with me. Donna will be delighted. The car is this way."

He picked up her two modest bags and strode along so fast that Gail had to trot to keep up with him. By the time she reached him, he was stowing the suitcases in a beautiful maroon-colored station wagon, with gold-painted letters on the side that read, "La Casa Manana."

He swung open the door for Gail and helped her in. He slid his long, lean body beneath the wheel, started the car, wheeled it out of the parking lot and headed it east along a broad highway.

Gail swallowed and asked huskily, "When will Larry be back?"

Troy Benton's dark face was inscrutable.

"Hard to say," he replied. "Maybe a few days, maybe a few months."

Gail stared at him in shocked dismay.

"But—didn't he get my telegram?" she asked.

Troy slanted a dark, derisive glance at her and drawled, "Oh, yes, he got your message."

Gail blinked, because she was disturbed by this man's obvious hostility and unable to understand it.

"Then why didn't he wait for me?" she said and her chin quivered piteously.

Once more Troy gave her that dark, hostile glance.

"Oh, his plans were already made and it was too late to change them." His tone was not quite so derisive now, as though the sight of her tear-filled eyes, the quiver of her mouth had softened his mood. "And anyway, he was sure Donna, my sister, and I would look after you."

She fought down the threat of tears, and after a moment Troy looked at her curiously.

"Incidentally, you're not at all what I expected," he admitted. "I very nearly didn't speak to you, I was so sure you were not the right girl."

"I know," said Gail with a touching humility that made Troy frown. "Larry is so terribly good-looking and so dashing—"

"And so rich," Troy contributed dryly.

"Well, yes," Gail said reluctantly. "I suppose he is. But I never thought about that."

"I'll bet you didn't." Now there was no doubting the derision in his voice, and Gail's color rose and there was anger in her eyes.

"I really can't see why I should have to explain to you how I fell in love with Larry," she said hotly.

"Of course not. The interesting question is why Larry fell in love with you."

"That's hard for me to understand, too," she admitted with an honest self-appraisal that he found touching. "We met by accident."

"I'll bet!" Troy murmured so softly she couldn't be sure whether she should answer or not.

"I don't in the least understand why Larry should love me or want to marry me," she began again.

"But you're sure he does?"

For a moment she was so taken by surprise that she could only look at him helplessly.

"Well, I'd hardly be here like this if I wasn't sure, would I?" she answered his question with another.

Troy said dryly, "That's a good question. I only wish I had a good answer."

Gail drew a long, hard breath, her hands twisted tightly together in the lap of her rumpled green print dress.

"We were in college together."

"And you think it very odd that he wants to marry me?"

"Frankly, and not wanting to hurt your feelings, Gail, I'm afraid I do," said Troy flatly. "Larry's girls are usually glamorous and sophisticated; not little girls who look as if they'd run away from home."

"I didn't run away. My aunt went to Europe, and she didn't think it was necessary for her to take me with her. When Larry was in Kentucky in the spring for the sale of his uncle's racing stables, he fell in love with me and asked me to marry him —some day. We didn't think then I'd ever be free

—I'm under such heavy obligations to my aunt. Then she and her friends found out about this cruise, designed especially for the elderly and the physically handicapped, and wanted to go. So that left me free to come and marry Larry."

Obviously the whole explanation was so simple from her viewpoint, that it left no room for argument. Troy could only glance at her, his jaw hardening, before he turned his attention once more to the road ahead of him.

"So now you see, Mr. Benton," said Gail when the silence grew awkward, "why I just sent Larry a telegram and came on down."

"I can see a great many things, I'm afraid, Gail," said Troy grimly, and turned from the broad Tamiami Trail down a side road that ended at a big white ranch house, with acres of grazing land, dotted with sleek, plump cattle.

Gail looked about her with eager appreciation.

"Oh, is this where Larry lives?" she asked.

"This is where my sister and I live," Troy told her, as he brought the car to a halt and got out to swing open the gate leading into the home grounds. "This is where you are to stay until we decide what to do with you."

His tone was dry, without expression, and Gail stiffened slightly, as though she found something offensive in it.

"That's something you won't have to worry

about, Mr. Benton," she told him swiftly. "As soon as Larry gets back, we'll be married and he'll take me off your hands. I could just as easily go to a hotel until he gets back, if it's a bother to you to have me here."

Troy eyed her as he got out of the car and swung the door open on her side. There was no hint of softening in his manner or in his tone as he said brusquely, "I take orders from Larry, and my orders were to bring you here, for as long as you want to stay."

A low white wall enclosed a patio at the end of the drive, and the green gate set in it swung open as a very pretty girl in her mid-twenties, clad in a blue-checked gingham play-suit, came to meet them. Her hair was thick and black and cut short, frothing over her head in lustrous curls. She was tanned and healthy-looking. As she came to them her dark eyes swept to Gail and suddenly she brought up short, her dark eyes widening.

"Oh, but, Troy, this isn't—this can't be—" she protested, and put a swift hand over her mouth.

"Oh, but it is, Donna my dear." Troy's tone was faintly acrid. "Gail, this is my sister, Donna. And, Donna, this is Gail Harrison, Larry's fiancée."

There was a brief but perceptible hesitation before he spoke the word, and the implications of that hesitation struck Gail hard. But she tilted her chin defiantly and met the other girl's wide eyes politely.

"How do you do, Miss Benton?" She said like a small, well-brought-up child.

"I'm not Miss Benton, Gail. I'm Mrs. Binford, a widow, though I am Troy's sister," said Donna, and glanced at Troy, who was busying himself removing Gail's modest luggage from the station wagon. "Do come in and let me show you to your room."

There was a sudden childish shriek of anger from behind the patio wall, and Donna flung up her hands in dismay.

"Oh, my sainted aunt, the babes are at it again! Excuse me, Gail, while I separate them and assay the damage they've done each other."

She ran back through the gate, and as it swung, Gail saw two small children: a boy not more than two or three, naked save for microscopic bathing trunks, and a girl perhaps a year younger clad in training pants. Both were sun-tanned, plump, handsome children, and the boy was busily banging his sister with the shovel from his beach bucket.

Donna separated the children, who continued to roar with rage.

Gail walked to the gate and stood watching, delighted, as Donna brought about an armistice between the two children and then came back to Gail.

"Are they yours?" Gail barely breathed the

18

question, and Donna looked at her as though startled at the depth of emotion in Gail's voice.

"Are you fond of children?" Donna asked when she had acknowledged the babes.

'Wide-eyed, Gail asked, "Isn't everybody? They're adorable."

"Occasionally," Donna admitted. "But everybody doesn't adore children! Our cook, who is a genius at cooking, loathes children, and the babes are terrified of her. Come along; let me get you settled before warfare breaks out again. It does about every twenty minutes, I have to admit."

Gail followed Donna to the house, but paused to look back at the children who were now playing as though never in their lives had they screamed at each other or fought.

Chapter Two

Gail unpacked and hung up her cherished trousseau in the wardrobes on either side of the dressing table. She sniffed appreciatively at the cedar lining of the two wardrobes and wished she had enough clothes to fill them. But her suitcase yielded up only enough to make a very feeble showing.

She wasn't quite sure what she would wear for dinner; uneasily, she finally selected a sheath of pale pink that the saleswoman had assured her was "exactly right" for Florida. When she had showered and dressed, she studied herself in the mirror of the dressing table and hoped she looked pretty enough to make Troy Benton feel that, after all, Larry had not made too big a mistake in choosing her.

She was very hungry when she finally left her

room. In the hall she heard wild screams from the children, splashing, and Donna's voice rising above it all. Instinctively she moved toward the sound and came to the nursery, a delightful place with a mural of fat, sassy-looking animals surrounding two small beds. Her attention centered on the open door leading into the bathroom. It was from this spot that the childish cries of glee, the laughter and the splashing were coming.

She paused in the doorway, filling her eyes with the picture of the two children splashing happily in a bathtub, each with a soapy washcloth, while Donna struggled to get the little girl to leave the water.

Donna looked up as Gail paused in the doorway, and with the back of her wet hand pushed back a curl that had tumbled across her forehead.

"Oh, is it dinner time?" Donna asked wearily. "These brats! First I have almost to beat them to get them into the tub, and then I have to threaten to drown them to get them out. Cissy, if you hit Buddy one more time, I'm going to spank the livin' daylights out of you! Buddy! Stop that!"

She looked up once more at Gail, grimacing as the little girl's soapy body slipped eel-like from between her hands.

"I need four hands at the very least," she confessed, "one pair to hold each of them."

"Let me help—please!" Gail begged, and came swiftly forward.

Once more Donna brushed the curl out of her eyes and looked at Gail's pretty pink sheath.

"Oh, no, you're all dressed up. They'll drown you," she protested, but it was plain she was tempted.

"That doesn't matter. The saleswoman said this was a drip-dry dress. I'd love to help you," Gail coaxed so sincerely that Donna stood up, reached for an enormous bath towel and pinned it about Gail's waist.

"All right, you asked for it," she said darkly, and turned back to the tub. "Now let's synchronize. I'll grab Buddy, because he's the hardest to hold and it takes experience; you grab Cissy and whatever you do—hang on tight!"

Gail laughed. "You make them sound like little animals," she protested.

Donna's eyebrows went up. "And they're not?"

"They're darlings, and you know it."

Donna, still eying the splashing, crowing, happy babies, nodded.

"They are, and I adore them, and I wouldn't take a million dollars apiece, tax free, for them. But there are times when I'd like to run away." She broke off as her voice shook.

"Oh, well," she went on briskly after a moment, "Here we go, Ready? Remember, now. You're to grab Cissy. Leave Buddy to me. One! Two! Three! Go!"

She reached for a small, fat, wriggling boy and

hung on despite his struggles to free himself; and Gail captured the small girl, who ceased struggling and looked up at Gail with wide, deep blue eyes set in a chubby small face.

"Hang on, Gail," urged Donna, briskly toweling the little boy, one eye on Gail and the girl. "She's a slippery critter and you have to ride herd on her."

But the child was obviously fascinated by Gail and sat quietly while Gail toweled her dry and slid her into her tiny sleeping suit.

"Oh, she's a lambie pie, and a sweetie," Gail crooned as she cradled the child and hid her nose for a moment against Cissy's soft neck. "Oh, don't babies smell delicious?" she burst out happily.

Donna, struggling to insert unwilling legs and arms into a sleeping suit, stared at her and barely managed to keep Buddy from sliding off her lap.

"You really are fond of youngsters, aren't you?" she asked slowly.

"I adore them, but I've never been around them much," Gail had to admit. "My aunt and her friends were all elderly spinsters, except for Miss Susie who was a widow. None of them had children, and I was so busy looking after Aunt Louisa I didn't have much chance to get acquainted with them."

"From the way you handled Cissy, I had an idea you were your neighborhood's most sought-after baby sitter," Donna admitted and heaved a sigh as she got the little boy into his night attire and lifted him. "Supper now, kids, and then off to beddie-bye!"

She hoisted the little boy to her shoulder, and Gail stood up, holding the little girl gently. Outside the bathroom, in the nursery, a table was waiting, and Gail and Donna put the children into their chairs.

"Think you can hold 'em down while I get their supper? Mary has it ready but she won't serve it," Donna said to Gail.

"Of course I can take care of them." Gail laughed, drew up a small rocker, and settled herself. "I'll tell them a story while you're gone."

The two children were staring at her with round, fascinated eyes when Donna came back a few minutes later with a laden tray. She and Gail fed the two children, and Donna's eyes on Gail were oddly speculative when at last the children had been tucked beneath their covers and Donna bent to drop a light kiss on the cheek of each one before she turned out the light and guided Gail out of the room.

"Hi, you've got quite a way with the babes," Donna said with frank admiration as they walked down the hall toward the living room.

"I'd like to have at least a dozen of my own," Gail told her.

"Well, whatever you do, don't drop a hint to Larry. He's terrified of children. Buddy swarmed

24

up his leg one day when he stopped by here, and Larry turned as white as a ghost and yelled for somebody to 'remove the brat.' You'd have thought a rattlesnake was attacking him." Donna checked herself guiltily and went on hurriedly, "the trouble with me is I talk too much. It would be different, of course, if Larry had children of his own."

They had reached the living room, where Troy was waiting for them with a pitcher of iced Martinis. He filled three glasses, offered one to Gail and one to Donna.

Gail hesitated, then accepted the cocktail. Donna sipped hers with a sigh.

"I needed that!" she admitted.

"Why you let the babes get you down—" Troy began.

"Well, it wasn't so bad tonight. I had help. Gail took over Cissy. You won't believe it, but there wasn't a yip out of Cissy when Gail scooped her out of the tub, scrubbed her dry and got her into her nightshirt. She's quite a gal, our Gail! Here's to her."

She turned, laughing, and held her glass high. Gail, flushing, sipped at her cocktail and managed not to choke.

"Strong enough?" asked Troy politely.

"Oh, my goodness, yes," Gail answered, and blinked against tears as she took another sip.

"Perhaps you don't like Martinis?" suggested Troy politely.

"I don't know, I've never tasted one before."

Troy's eyebrows shot up, and the look in his eyes was derisive.

"Shall I get you something else? Scotch on the rocks, perhaps? We have some Bourbon and, of course, champagne, though that's for very special occasions," he drawled.

Donna, watching Gail, said sharply, "Shut up, Troy. Gail, how about some orange juice or tomato juice?"

"No, thanks, this was fine," said Gail humbly, and put down the glass from which she had taken two small sips.

The appearance of a woman in the dining room doorway startled Gail so that she could say no more. She could only stare. The woman was vast, well over two hundred pounds, and rather tall. Her skin was copper-colored and there were golden hoops in her ears. She wore a voluminous dress over many petticoats, and in hue the dress was a weird mingling of every color in the spectrum. Around the woman's neck there were literally dozens of strands of beads, ranging from short ones that hugged her ample neck to others that fell to her waist.

The woman's eyes were dark, and she swung them from Troy to Donna and then to Gail.

"You eat now?" she demanded, her voice a low guttural.

Donna, who had not been aware of the woman's presence, gave a tiny start and turned swiftly.

"Oh, ah, yes, of course, Mary, We'll be right there," Donna said, and turned to Troy and Gail, drawing them with her across the room and into the dining room.

The table had been laid for three, and Mary was waiting as they reached it.

Donna said, "Mary, this is Miss Harrison who is visiting us."

The woman's eyes swept over Gail in the slim pink sheath.

"She too skinny. I fat um up," she said firmly, and walked out, the door swinging shut behind her.

Gail stared at Donna, who made a gesture of defensiveness.

"Pay her no mind, Gail," she sighed. "She is a Seminole, and her tribe is still at war with the United States."

Gail stared at Troy, who grinned at her amazed expression.

"It's quite true," he admitted. "Mary's tribe still maintain that since the United States captured Osceola under a flag of truce, they want no part of citizenship. Most of the other tribes in the Glades have settled their quarrel with the government and are accepting the profits. Mary's tribe is still holding out. So she cooks for us as a favor, and accepts the whopping salary we pay her as no more than her due."

"And what a cook she is!" breathed Donna, eying the door hungrily.

It swung open and Mary appeared, balancing a huge, well-filled tray.

She put down in front of Gail a small casserole from which an exquisitely tempting odor rose; to Donna she handed a plate of raw vegetables, a cored apple and two crackers.

Donna wailed, "Oh, come now, Mary. I want what Gail's having. I'm hungry, and that's your famous shrimp in cream sauce."

"You too fat," said Mary grimly. "You eat carrot sticks. She too skinny. She eat lots, get fat."

Beside Troy's place she placed a platter holding a sizzling steak, a baked potato dripping with butter, green beans and a tall glass of milk.

Donna gave a small, stricken moan. Gail looked swiftly at her and then at Troy, who was beginning his dinner with an excellent appetite, paying no attention to Donna's wails.

"Here, Donna, I've got twice as much as I can possibly eat." Gail pushed the small casserole toward Donna.

Behind her, a stern voice spoke sharply. "Miss Harrison!"

Guiltily Gail looked up at Mary, who was placing a dish of tossed salad beside her plate.

"Yes, Mary? I only meant that I can't possibly eat so much," Gail stammered.

Mary regarded her coolly, without favor.

"I must ask you not to interfere," stated Mary, her voice still guttural but her English perfect. "Miss Donna have very little will power. She worries because she has gained weight taking care of her children. She has asked me to help her keep on a diet. It would be easier to diet the children; at least I can take food away from them. But Miss Donna must be fed. And I am under strict orders to give her only what is on her diet list. You will be kind enough not to interfere."

She turned with a whirl of her floor-length, voluminous skirts and strode out of the room, her golden earrings swinging.

Gail stared after her, and then, her color high, she turned her head and met Donna's amused, slightly abashed eyes.

"She's telling the truth, Gail. I *do* want to take off a few pounds, and I love to eat, so my only hope was to get Mary to help me," Donna explained. "And don't be startled when she breaks out of her Indian talk. She speaks English as well as we do, better sometimes when it pleases her to. But because she knows most 'pale faces' expect Indians to grunt and say 'How,' it sometimes amuses her to live up to that picture."

Gail smiled shyly. "I don't think you're a bit too

fat, Donna. I'd love to be exactly your size. I think you're beautiful."

Troy glanced at Gail and then at Donna with a faint curl of his lip. But Donna accepted the compliment in the spirit in which it had been given.

"You're a sweetie-pie, Gaily honey, and thanks a heap." Donna smiled. "Trouble is, I'm bursting out of all my clothes and can't afford to buy any new ones. So the only hope is to get back my girlish figure."

"You know that's not quite true, Donna." Troy seemed offended. "I've told you to go buy whatever you need, because the family bankroll can be stretched to cover any reasonable extra expenses."

"You're a sweetie-pie, too, darling, and I love you to pieces," Donna assured him. "But you've done enough for me and the babes—taking us in, feeding, sheltering us, just because there was no insurance money after the babes' father died. Supplying me with a new wardrobe would be a mite too much."

Troy glanced at Gail, back to Donna and said curtly, "We needn't discuss the matter now, surely. After all, we have a guest who couldn't possibly be interested in our family squabbles."

His tone made Gail feel oddly uncomfortable, but she reminded herself that it would be only a few days until Larry came back and she would be able to leave.

"Tell us about yourself, Gail honey," urged

Donna. "What was it like up there in the 'horse country' of Kentucky? Must have been fabulous, all those gorgeous racing stables."

Gail smiled ruefully.

"I really wouldn't know about that," she admitted. Aunt Louisa didn't approve of racing and I never had time to go far enough away from home to see any of the horses, except for a few mares and their colts down in the pasture near our house. I used to sneak off down the bridle path between our house and the edge of the field to watch them. That's how I met Larry. He almost rode me down, and he was very angry with me for being in the way."

Once more Donna and Troy exchanged glances, and Donna began drawing Gail out, with interested questions and comments until, by the time dinner was over, Donna and Troy had a clear picture of Gail's life with Aunt Louisa.

When dinner was over and they moved into the big dining room for coffee, Donna said, "I'd better be sure the babes are all right."

Gail rose eagerly.

"Couldn't I do that? I'll tuck their covers close and be sure not to wake them, if you'll let me," she pleaded as though for some great boon.

Donna stared at her with raised eyebrows, then grinned and relapsed into her deep comfortable chair, one foot tucked under her as she reached for her coffee.

"Be my guest, do!" she urged with a slight wave of her hand. Gail laughed and slipped out of the room.

The children were sleeping soundly, and the room was not yet quite dark. Gail hung over them, her heart melting with tenderness for their vulnerability as they slept.

She went quietly back along the hall. Suddenly she stopped still, for Troy was speaking to Donna in a tone that was cold and harsh.

". . . a conniving little schemer," he was saying. "Oh, I grant you she does it very well. But no girl nowadays could possibly be as guileless, as ingenuous as she is pretending to be. Met Larry by accident! Ha! I just bet she did! She probably haunted that bridle path from the day she knew he was in town, feeling sure he would come that way sooner or later."

"But, Troy, a girl who was brought up as she says she was—" Donna began.

"That's just the point: brought up as she *says* she was! How do we know there's a word of truth in that fantastic yarn she spun for us?" Troy snorted. "Larry was one smart hombre when he took it on the lam the minute her wire came. And he's smart enough to stay away until I let him know she's gone."

Gail forced herself to move forward, to step into the living room. Troy and Donna looked up, abashed at the discovery that she had overheard them.

"I heard, of course," said Gail huskily, and sat down, because her knees were trembling. "I'm glad I did, because now you can tell me why Larry isn't here. I *have* to know."

Troy said grimly, "Yes, I think you do. Larry isn't here because you scared him into running."

"Oh, Troy, don't!" Donna pleaded.

"I scared Larry?" Gail managed after a moment.

"Well, you're not the first marriage-minded female who has scared Larry into running fast and far and staying there until the danger had passed," Troy told her harshly.

"Troy, please!" Donna cut in. But Gail put up a shaking hand to silence her, and her eyes held Troy's steadily.

"I think you'd better tell me everything," she said huskily.

"I think so, too," Troy agreed. "Frankly, Larry had forgotten your name. When the telegram came, he had the dickens of a time remembering where he had met you, until he looked at the name of the town where the telegram had been sent."

"Oh, but he wrote to me!" Gail protested.

"Oh, he wrote to you, did he?" Troy's eyes were suddenly wary and there was a sternness in his setting jaw that frightened her. "I suppose you brought the letters with you?"

"Well, of course," Gail answered, puzzled that he should ask such a question.

"And I suppose the letters are full of things like 'Darling, will you marry me'?" Troy persisted.

Color poured into Gail's face.

"No, there's nothing like that in the letters," she said huskily. "We knew when he left Starkville that I would never be able to marry him because of Aunt Louisa. I couldn't walk out on her after all she'd done for me. So Larry and I just wrote friendly letters."

Desperately embarrassed, she looked from Troy to Donna.

"At least Larry's were just friendly," she confessed. "I'd never had anybody to love, and I guess mine were love letters."

"But his were not?" Troy demanded.

"Oh, no," she said humbly.

"Then if you have no love letters from him—and nobody, I'm quite sure, heard him say he wanted to marry you, according to what you've told us of your life in Starkville—you really have no grounds whatever for filing a suit, have you?" Troy demanded sharply.

Deeply puzzled, Gail repeated, "Filing a suit? I don't understand."

"Oh, come off it, Gail! You're not that simple," snapped Troy. "A suit for breach of promise, of course. Such suits are illegal in Florida, anyway; but I suppose you thought you could threaten him with a scandal—as if Larry would care a hang about that—and he'd pay you off. Well, let me tell you here and now, my girl: you're wasting your time pursuing Larry."

Gail listened to him, shrinking farther and farther back into her chair, until suddenly she gave a little moan and covered her face with her hands.

"Shut up, Troy!" snapped Donna, and went to Gail, perching on the arm of her chair, her arm about the girl's shaking shoulders. "Don't pay any attention to him, honey."

"She'd better pay attention to me," Troy insisted savagely. "I have Larry's orders to put her on the bus in the morning and send her back home."

Gail gave a small, stricken cry and her hands dropped from her tear-wet face.

"But I can't, she said. "I haven't any place to go!"

"Your aunt—" Troy began.

"She's abroad, I don't quite know where," stammered Gail, and there was panic in her eyes. "She said she'd done enough for me; that it was time I was shifting for myself. But I don't have any training. Oh, what am I going to do?"

It was a small, childish wail of terror and panic, but Troy was adamant.

"I don't know what you're going to do. I only know what you're *not* going to do, and that is bilk Larry for a handsome settlement. Not but what he could afford it easily enough, but I refuse to stand by and watch you do it."

Donna turned on him furiously.

"*Will* you shut up?" she blazed so hotly that Troy looked faintly staggered. "Leave her alone, will you? She's worn out from that long trip, and now you've beat her over the head with the truth about Larry, who's a rat and a skunk, even if he is rich as mud and handsome as the devil. Let the girl get a good night's sleep, and tomorrow we can make plans. But now shut up and leave her alone."

Troy said defensively, "I only felt she should know that Larry wasn't fooled by her conniving little act any more than we were."

"Speak for yourself, you lug," snapped Donna. "I believe her! I think she's strictly on the level and every word she's said is the solemn truth. Now you be quiet and let me get her to bed."

Donna urged Gail to her feet and, with an arm about her, guided her out of the living room and down the hall to the bedroom assigned to her.

Chapter Three

It was late the following morning before Gail awoke.

She dressed swiftly in the rumpled green print she had worn on the trip down. She could hear the happy squealing of the children in the patio, and she had a sudden urge to slip away without seeing anyone. Hastily, with shaking hands, she repacked her bag and straightened. There was a gentle tap at the door. It opened, and Donna poked her head in, smiling. Her smile faded as she saw Gail dressed for traveling, and the packed suitcase being snapped shut.

"Oh, Gail, honey, you're not leaving?" she protested as she came into the room.

"I have to," said Gail huskily. "I couldn't possibly stay any longer, now that I know Larry won't come back until I'm gone."

"Well, at least you aren't leaving until you've

had some breakfast," said Donna firmly, and linked her arm in Gail's. "Come on out to the patio, where I can keep an eye on the babes, and Mary will bring you some breakfast. It's nice out there this morning. Birds singing their fool heads off, and the like of that."

It *was* nice, Gail told herself as she sat down at the small, glass-topped table, and the children beamed joyously at her from their sand pile behind its neat low border.

Mary came out, carrying a tray which she deposited on the table, and stood back, her dark, inscrutable eyes holding an almost friendly light as she lifted one huge hand and growled a guttural, "How!"

Gail managed to drag up a faint smile and lifted her own hand, saying, "And how to you, too!"

Mary did not quite smile. But her copper-colored face indicated that she was faintly amused as she turned and went away.

"Aren't you having breakfast?" Gail asked Donna, seeing that the tray was arranged for only one.

"Oh, I had breakfast early in the day," Donna said lightly. "The babes see to that. If one of them ever slept past five-thirty, the shock would be more than I could endure. I'll sit with you and have another cup of coffee while you eat."

"I'm not very hungry," Gail said huskily.

"Gail, unless you clean up every single scrap of

the food on that tray, s'help me, I'll paddle you!" said Donna sternly. "The man hasn't been born yet who's worth a girl going hungry! Certainly not Larry Stillman. Now eat your breakfast, there's a good girl."

Obediently, Gail sipped the orange juice, and found her appetite growing as she moved on to the scrambled eggs and crisp bacon.

Donna poured a cup of coffee, lit a cigarette and studied Gail unobtrusively through its thin blue smoke. It was obvious that she had something on her mind and was skirting about trying to find a way to express it.

"Look, Gail, have you made up your mind what you're going to do?" she asked at last, unable to find a more gentle way to begin.

Gail put down her fork and very carefully laid the bit of toast she had just buttered beside it. Her pretty mouth quivered and there was a mist of tears in her eyes.

"Just go away somewhere, so Larry can come home," she said through her teeth.

"Come home my foot!" said Donna vigorously. "Have you any idea how much time he spends here? About two weeks a year, and then only if he has La Casa stacked with house guests."

Gail said huskily, "But I've got to go somewhere, find a job—"

"Without any training at all?"

"You don't think maybe I could get a job?"

"Honey, in these days of highly specialized training, believe me, there's practically no market for a girl who has had none whatever," Donna said gently. "It took me four years to become a legal secretary, and I studied law nights for two years to get to be really good at my job."

Gail looked at her, appalled. Panic once more registered in her eyes.

Donna said, as she brushed the ash from her cigarette into a small glass tray beside her, "I've been thinking. There is one thing that you're obviously very good at."

Gail asked breathlessly, "What, Donna?"

Donna gestured toward the children.

"You are obviously fond of children and you have a way with them," she said, and was silent, watching Gail's expressive face, the sudden light that came into her eyes.

"Oh, Donna," she breathed, "do you think I could get a job as a children's nursemaid?"

Donna asked frankly, "The thought doesn't shock you?"

Bewildered, Gail asked, "Why should it shock me? It's a lovely thought. Oh, Donna, if I only could!"

Donna beamed at her in relief.

"Honey, you've got one, if you really want it!" she said happily.

Still bewildered, Gail said, "I don't understand."

Donna leaned toward her eagerly.

"Look I adore the babes! They are utterly precious and I'm crazy about them," she began. "But I *do* feel that for me to settle down here with poor Troy and make him support us, when I've got a very good profession and could earn an excellent salary that would provide for all our expenses and leave a few dollars over to save for their education, is not right. And to be brutally honest about it, I loved my job; I'd be even crazier about the babes if I could turn them over to someone else, five days a week. How does that sound to you?"

"It sounds wonderful, Donna, unbelievable!" Gail gasped.

Donna beamed at her happily.

"That's the way it sounds to me, too," she confessed. "And if you like the idea, then you've got a job."

Gail looked at the children, squatting in their sand pile, absorbed in some game of their own devising, then looked back at Donna uneasily.

"But what would Troy say?" she asked.

Donna grinned wryly. "Oh, Troy's all for it. Oh, not as enthusiastically as I am, of course, but then that's not to be expected," she admitted. "He thinks a mother's place is in the home looking after her children, even if she is a widow and has their future to consider."

"I didn't mean that," Gail insisted huskily. "I

mean the things he thinks about me; the feelings he has that I'm a 'conniving schemer.' "

"Oh, that!" Donna brushed it aside as though it were of no importance whatever. "You'll just have to convince him that you are nothing of the sort. He's not any too sure now; not after the talking-to I gave him last night, anyway."

Still Gail hesitated, but Donna saw the look in her eyes as she watched the children at their game.

"You see, Gail honey, I've done a bit of spare-time work for a very nice guy in Grove City," Donna went on persuasively. "He likes my work; my kind of executive legal secretary isn't easily come by down here. He likes the idea that I can be of real assistance, run the office, handle clients, look after things in general when he has to be out of town. He's offered me an excellent salary, but I couldn't take it, tempted as I was, because of the babes. I'm not willing to hand them over to just any baby sitter that comes along; I have to *know* they are with someone who loves them and who'll give them loving attention and care. I'd given up hope of finding such a person. But the way you handled Cissy last night, the way she and Buddy took to you at first, sight, fairly gladdened my heart, if I may coin a phrase. You'd be simply a part of the family, my trusted and honored assistant, and I'd treat you like a beloved sister! You'd have a good salary, room and board and all the privileges of home. How does it sound to you?"

Gail drew a deep, hard breath and lifted her head, her eyes shining.

"It sounds wonderful!" she breathed.

As Mary came back to the patio for the breakfast things, Donna told her joyously, "Congratulate me, Mary. Miss Harrison's going to stay and look after the babes so I can take that job Colonel Jordan offered me."

"What's Mr. Troy going to say about that?" asked Mary dryly, as she loaded the breakfast dishes on her tray.

Gail said uneasily, "I'm afraid he won't like it, and if he doesn't then I can't do it."

"Like fun you can't!" snapped Donna briskly. "If he doesn't like it, you and I and the babes will move into town and find a bungalow."

Mary's smile was faintly sardonic.

"You think that will scare him?" she asked. She picked up the tray and went back into the house. Donna glared after her.

"That proves it," she said curtly. "I have suspected for a long time that she eavesdropped on everything that was said in the house, and now I'm convinced of it."

"If Troy doesn't want me here, Donna, you know I can't stay," Gail insisted.

"Well, you heard what I told her," Donna said firmly. "If he doesn't want you here, then we'll move into town."

"I couldn't let you do that just on my account,

Donna," Gail protested, and looked at the children, plump and brown as berries, happily absorbed in their sand pile. "I couldn't let you give up all this lovely space and the children's wellbeing just to create a job for me."

"Who's creating—" Donna began.

"You are, Donna," Gail cut in. "You know as well as I do that you are offering me a job just out of charity."

"Charity my foot!" snapped Donna. "Look, you blessed idiot, didn't you listen when I told you that I was aching to get back to work? I'll mildew if I have to sit here day after day and keep the babes from slaughtering each other. And that's the main part of my job. Mary won't allow me in the kitchen, and if I try to do any housework she comes right in behind me and does it over again, sniffing at the way I did it. I'd fire her if she'd let me! But she won't. She's devoted to Troy and has worked for him for years; and the babes and I only moved in a year ago. She adores Troy, but she only tolerates me."

As if to bring a point to the discussion, Buddy lifted his sandshovel and brought it down smartly on Cissy's blonde head. For a moment Cissy was silent with surprise, then she gave vent to a roar of fury and flung herself upon her brother.

"See what I mean?" Donna sighed as she stood up. But Gail was ahead of her, and had scooped the furiously howling Cissy from the sandpile and was cuddling her in her arms, while Buddy looked on, scowling. Cissy stopped in the middle of a roar, stared at Gail and then, her small face completely dry of tears, smiled enchantingly and tucked herself more firmly into Gail's arms.

"Aren't you ashamed, Buddy, to hit your little sister?" Gail scolded him gently. "Don't you know little brothers are supposed to protect their sisters, not to go around hitting them? You want to grow up and be a fine young man, don't you?"

Donna said at her shoulder, "You're wasting your time appealing to his better nature, Gail honey, because at his age, he hasn't developed one yet. He's just a small animal, and it will take time to make him learn he's anything else."

Briskly, matter of factly, Donna up-ended the small, truculent boy, gave his round bottom a firm smack and said, "There! Now you see how it hurts. And every time you hit Cissy, you'll get spanked. Do you understand me?"

Buddy started to roar, gave his mother a wary glance, then smiled sweetly.

"*Pretty* Mommie," he said tenderly.

Donna stared at him and then at Gail, who was holding Cissy; Cissy looked down at Buddy, an unbearably smug expression on her small face.

"I ask you," said Donna, and set the boy on his feet once more. "How in blazes can you spank him when he gives you that look of dewy-eyed innocence and murmurs sweet nothings?"

She watched the little boy, who had returned to his play as though nothing had happened. Then she turned to Gail, and there were tears in her eyes.

"I might be able to handle him better if he wasn't the spitting image of his father," she said huskily. "When he looks at me like that, I can just see Dennis after he'd forgotten something important. He'd just give me that lopsided grin, his eyes as blue as October skies and his voice like melted honey, and say, 'Honey, I'm sorry. Forgive me? Because I love you.'"

She turned sharply away, and Gail knelt beside the sand pile and set Cissy beside Buddy. Gail remained with the children for a little while, giving Donna a chance to recover her self-control. When Donna came back to the sand pile, Gail smiled shyly up at her.

"So you think I offered you a job out of charity, do you?" she mocked ruefully. "Do you begin to see how badly I need you?"

"I'd love to stay, but only if Troy doesn't mind, and if it doesn't keep Larry away from his home," Gail said.

Donna was silent for a moment, and then she chuckled dryly.

"Want to know where Larry is?"

Gail's eyes widened. "Why—yes, I suppose I do."

"He sailed from Miami at midnight, aboard a

yacht loaded with free-loaders, and without an itinerary. 'Who cares? Wherever there isn't a war let's go.' If he comes back in six months or a year, I'll be very surprised," Donna said flatly.

Gail's color rose. "Then he didn't go just because I wired him I was on my way?"

Donna shook her head. "He only moved up the departure date," she answered. "He's been planning this cruise for quite a while. He was in no particular hurry, until your wire came. And then —well there was a pretty frantic rush to get his guests aboard. Some are joining him in Jamaica; a few flew down from New York. Sailing time was scheduled for midnight last night."

Gail listened, her mouth set in a thin line, her eyes dark with misery. When Donna had finished, she looked up at her, and said huskily, "I've been an awful fool, haven't I?"

"No, honey," said Donna quietly. "Just young and inexperienced. Being young is something time will take care of; and being inexperienced is something that will also pass away. You haven't been a fool at all—you've just been young. And Larry, drat the guy, is a charmer from the word go!"

Gail nodded soberly and sat silent for a long moment.

Donna watched her, and there was tenderness in her eyes.

"Honey, you and I and Troy are going to have ourselves a fine time, and you're going to forget

Larry Stillman ever lived," she said gently. "I have always wanted a sister, and Troy was always too busy getting through college, and then putting this place on its feet, to find time to marry. But now that I can support myself and the babes, he'll be able to take free breath; and maybe he and Ellen Matthews can make some plans for their future. She's a very sweet girl; you'll like her."

"Troy is engaged?" asked Gail.

"Well, let's say he and Ellen have been going together since about the Year One," said Donna lightly. "But Ellen has had a heavy job looking after an invalid mother and a father who is as charming as he is feckless! And this past year, since Ellen's mother died, Troy has had the babes and me on his shoulders and has, I'm sure, hesitated to ask Ellen to come here to live with us all! But who knows? Now that I'm going to be earning my own and the babes' living, something may really develop."

"If only he won't mind my staying on!" said Gail uneasily.

"Well, he'll be home for lunch and we can settle that immediately," Donna said. "And after lunch, you and I can drive in town and you can have your baptism of fire by trying to keep the babes in order while I go talk to Bob Jordan."

Chapter Four

Gail was on the patio, supervising the children's play, when Troy came home for lunch. In a thin blue cotton frock left over from summer, her hair tumbled about her flushed, laughing face as she bent over the children, she made a very pretty picture.

For a moment Troy studied her, the children, the setting. Then he went on into the house, and Gail drew a deep breath and returned to the job of amusing the children.

It seemed to her an age-long time before Donna came out. Donna's mouth was set in a firm line and there was determination in her chin. But as Gail looked up, anxiety approaching terror in her eyes, Donna laughed.

"Goodness, honey, don't you look as though

you were being doomed to a firing squad," she laughed.

Gail stood up and carefully brushed the sand from her hands.

"He doesn't want me here."

"He wants to talk to you."

"He needn't. I'll go quietly," Gail tried very hard for a light tone that was not at all convincing.

"Pooh! I told you what we'd do if he was stubborn."

"And I told you I wouldn't let you!"

Donna smiled and said lightly, "Go and talk to him, Gail, and then we'll decide. Run along now. He won't bite you, I promise. And if he gets sassy, you sass him right back. He'll love it."

Gail drew a deep, hard breath and tilted her chin. She walked past Donna without another word and into the house.

She found Troy in the big living room, standing at one of the windows, his hands jammed hard in the pockets of his khaki riding breeches. His khaki-colored shirt was open at his strong, sun-bronzed throat, and his sleeves were rolled above his elbows. He looked, she told herself as he turned to face her, almost as much like an Indian as Mary.

"Good morning," he greeted her curtly. "Donna tells me that you are willing to stay on and help her with the children."

"Not if you'd rather I didn't," Gail told him huskily.

"It's Donna's decision, not mine."

"But I'd be here in the house when you came home. And I know how much you hate me."

Troy scowled at her. "I don't hate you. That's silly. I admit that I don't approve of your behavior, running off down here to see Larry without any assurance at all that he still wanted to marry you," he pointed out grimly. "But that's your business. If Donna wants to go back to work, and you are willing to be a nursemaid for the children—"

"I've been a nursemaid for my aunt ever since I can remember," Gail reminded him. "The children are darlings, and taking care of them will be fun. But if I'm unwelcome, unwanted here, I'd much rather go away and find some other job. And I can. I haven't had any training, but I'm young and strong and there must be somebody somewhere who needs what I can offer."

Troy studied her with a curious intentness before he spoke.

"Donna's been very unhappy since Dennis, her husband, died," he said slowly. "She's got some crazy idea that she and the children should not be dependent on me, which is pretty silly. But then, women are funny people. I know she'd be much happier back at the job she does so well, but I know, too, that she'd never make the move if she

51

weren't sure the children were well cared for. She seems to feel she can trust you."

The coldness that had gripped her heart melted a little and color came back slowly to her pale face.

"Then I may stay?" she asked faintly.

"As long as Donna wants you, of course."

Gail drew a long, deep breath and her hands clenched tightly.

"I won't ever let you be sorry, Mr. Benton."

"I hope not." He didn't seem to sure of that. "And the name is Troy, Gail."

To her surprise and delight he smiled at her and thrust out his hand.

"Welcome aboard, Gail," he said. "Glad to have you with us."

"*Oh.*" Gail's voice shook, and her hand in his was clammy with excitement. "Oh, thank you!"

Troy laughed slightly.

"You sound as if I'd just given you a mink coat and a pass key to the mint," he drawled teasingly.

"You've given me a lot more than that," she insisted earnestly. "You've given me a job and a home, just when I thought I was never going to have either. Oh, Mr. Benton—I mean Troy—I'll take such good care of the babies, and I'll keep out of your way. I promise I won't bother you."

Troy's eyes had warmed faintly, although some instinct told her that he was not yet completely won over.

"That's rather a large order," he said dryly. "Not bothering me, I mean. I have a hunch you're going to bother the blazes out of me before you're through."

Gail digested that, puzzled, trying to understand, and then she asked uneasily, "Do you think *he* will mind me staying on?"

Some of the friendliness vanished from Troy's eyes.

"You mean Larry?" he asked unnecessarily. "I see no reason why he should. After all, I merely manage his properties for him. This place and a large section of the land belong to me. Larry's place is a couple of miles farther along the Tamiami Trail."

"Then my staying on wouldn't prevent him from coming home if he wanted to?" Gail persisted.

Troy smiled faintly. "I can see no reason why it should. Larry doesn't consider *La Casa Mañana* home, in any sense. He's got a suite at a hotel on Miami Beach; an apartment in New York; a cottage at Palm Springs. But mostly he uses the yacht as a basis of operations. I tried to persuade him to hang onto that racing stable in Kentucky, but Larry has a horror of being tied down to anything or anybody."

Gail nodded thoughtfully. "I guess I don't know him very well," she admitted honestly.

"I'm quite sure of that," Troy told her, and now

his eyes were cool again. "Well, then, that's settled. You're to stay on and look after the children, and Donna will take the job a pal of mine, Bob Jordan, has been trying to give her for a year. So shall we have lunch now? I've got to get back to work."

"I'll go look after the children while Donna has lunch."

"Oh, no, you won't," Donna said briskly from the doorway. "I've given the babes their lunch and they are bedded down for a nap. We'll all have lunch, and then, Gail, you'll help me stuff the babes into clean clothes and we'll go into town. I can't wait to tell Bob he's got a new executive secretary. And then, of course, I'll have to do some shopping."

"But of course," said Troy dryly, a twinkle in his eyes as he watched his sister's flushed, excited face and bright eyes.

"Well, why not? I can't very well slither about Bob's office, being impressive as anything, in shorts or a playsuit, can I?" Donna argued.

Gail was blissfully content merely to sit and listen as they rattled gaily on.

Finally Troy laughed and thrust back his chair.

"We're holding an auction at three, and I'd better get going. The calf crop was pretty good this year, and we're disposing of half of them," he announced. "See you at dinner."

When he had gone, Gail drew a deep breath and beamed at Donna.

"He's going to let me stay," she said shakily.

"Well, you little goop, of course he is." Donna seemed surprised. "Didn't I tell you he'd be delighted?"

Gail's smile was wry.

"Well, I didn't see any sign of his being delighted, but I'll settle for his just being willing," she said.

Donna said gently, "Honey, don't be so humble! You don't *have* to be, a girl as lovely and as sweet as you are! You'll be the light of the house, and I'll be willing to bet you that within a month, Ellen Matthews will be riding over here to scratch your eyes out—in a nice, lady-like way, of course. Ellen *is* a lady, even if she can lose her temper and swear like a trooper. Running a fishing camp, with a father who just doesn't give a hang whether they make money or not, isn't exactly conducive to a Lady Vere de Vere manner. But Ellen's a very good scout and you'll like her."

"Even while she's scratching my eyes out?" Gail laughed, and asked curiously, "Why would she want to do that, anyway?"

"Why? Are you being coy? Or would you really like to know?"

Puzzled, Gail answered honestly, "I really would like to know."

"Well, then, because Ellen's never had any

competition in her pursuit of Troy, and now that you are here under the same roof with him——" She broke off as Gail's eyes flew wide and a warm tide of crimson crept over her face. "Well, do you begin to get the picture?"

"Oh, that's perfectly ridiculous!" Gail gasped. "Why, Troy doesn't even like me."

Mary came into the room, a list in her hand, and eyed the two sternly.

"Are you planning to spend the whole afternoon here?" she wanted to know with deceptive mildness. "It's my afternoon off, and I'd like to clear the table before I leave. And here's the grocery list."

Donna stood up guiltily and smiled placatingly at Mary.

"Sorry, Mary, we were just gabbing," she said, and took the list. "Sure you don't want to ride in town with us and prowl the supermarket?"

"Today," stated Mary firmly, "I go fishing with my family."

"Oh," said Donna, "that sounds like fun. I'll do the marketing, Mary, of course."

"Tonight we have fish for supper," said Mary firmly, and added, a faint gleam that might have been humor in her eyes, "For you, I broil them with lemon sauce."

"That sounds wonderful, Mary!" Donna answered gratefully.

At the doorway she hesitated, "I don't suppose,

Mary, you'd care to tell me where you're going to fish?"

Mary flung her a glance of outrage.

"You think I betray my tribe's secret?" she asked haughtily.

"No, of course not, Mary; forget I asked!"

"I forget you asked," said Mary, and began clearing the table.

As they went on to the nursery, Donna said, "Oh, Gail, honey, I'm so glad you're staying! It's going to be wonderful to have you here. Troy's a lamb and I adore him; but I do get lonely for 'girl talk.'"

"I'm so glad I can stay!" Gail answered radiantly. "I'm so glad Troy doesn't mind!"

Donna laughed. As Buddy awoke, she began briskly the task of getting the children up and dressed, with Gail helping enthusiastically.

Donna's car was a small Dauphine into which the four of them fitted cozily, and as they drove toward town, Gail looked out of the window, Cissy snuggled in her lap, and reflected on the difference between this journey and the one she had made yesterday with Troy. Then she had been bewildered and uneasy because Larry had not been at the bus station to greet her. Also, Troy's behavior had told her that she was unwelcome and that he wanted to be rid of her as soon as possible. But today she felt snug and secure in the knowledge that Donna wanted her, the children needed her, and Troy had said, "Welcome aboard, Gail. Glad to have you here."

Once they were in the small, pretty town with its palm-shaded streets and its neat, pastel-colored stucco houses behind impossibly green lawns, Donna found a parking space and drew a deep breath, her cheeks flushed, her eyes bright.

"Well, Gail, this is it," she said gaily. "Do I look like a gal hunting a job?"

"You look like a gal any employer would welcome with open arms and a handsome pay check," Gail responded.

Donna patted her knee, kissed Cissy, gave Buddy a caressing touch and said, "I won't be long."

"I'team," said Cissy, bright-eyed.

"Oh, sure, ice-cream by all means. Why not," demanded Donna, "especially now that you are all dressed up in your best bib and tucker? Chocolate ice-cream should look very well on that pinafore, don't you think, Gail?"

Gail hugged the small, blonde child in the pale blue chambray pinafore and answered, "Oh, I won't let her spill any on herself."

"Oh, golly," breathed Donna, "do *you* have something to learn about kids! *Wowee!*"

"I'team," Cissy insisted.

"Wait until Mommie gets back, and then we'll have ice-cream all around, Baby," Donna promised. "That is, unless you cry now. If you do, nobody gets ice-cream."

Cissy hesitated, then gave her mother an entrancing grin that revealed tiny, rice-like teeth and nodded.

"If she cries, Mommie, I'll smack her," Buddy promised cheerfully.

"You do, and I'll smack you when I get back, my fine-feathered friend," Donna threatened darkly, and slid out of the car.

Gail watched her cross the street in the blazing sunlight—a slender, very pretty woman in a thin, cool-looking white sunback dress, her high heels clicking merrily. A dark doorway into the lobby of a two-storied building swallowed her, and Gail and the children turned to watch the traffic and the pedestrians.

"Mary!" announced Buddy as a Seminole woman in a brilliantly patterned dress, tall, stately, a vast assortment of beads swinging about her neck, vast golden hoops in her ears swung past. But it was not Mary. As Gail assured Buddy of this, she noticed several other women in similar garb, all moving about the streets as much at home as though they were in their native Glades. There were a few older men as well, most of them wearing pants and shirts that were similar to those worn by the white men. But their copper-colored faces, as well as the arrogant self-assurance of their walk, set them apart.

Donna emerged from the building at last, but she was not alone. A tall, handsome, distinguished-looking man in his middle forties walked beside her, looking down into her lifted face, obviously charmed by her.

"Gail, honey," Donna reached the side of the parked car, "this is my boss, Robert Jordan. Bob, this is Gail Harrison who's visiting with us. We are hoping to keep her permanently."

"Hello, Gail," said Bob Jordan, and gripped her hand with a warm, friendly pressure. "Donna tells me that the only reason she can take the job I've been trying to give her for a year is that you are visiting. I'm intensely grateful; I have needed Donna very badly."

Donna said with unexpected gravity, "I hope you have, Bob."

Bob Jordan frowned as though he found that puzzling.

"Well, can you doubt it, for Pete's sake?" he asked. "You've given me what time you could spare. Surely you must have realized how desperately I needed somebody with your training and experience and how impossible it's been to find anybody."

Donna beamed at him radiantly. "Of course. I'm just being silly. I've wanted the job so badly, and had given up hope I'd be able to accept it until the babes grew up and went off the college or got married."

Bob laughed as he looked at the children, who were eying him with frank curiosity.

"Well, I'm certainly glad I needn't wait that long for an executive assistant," he said. "So thanks again, Gail, and a very warm welcome to our fair city."

"I'm very happy to be here, Mr. Jordan!" Gail assured him.

As Donna slid behind the wheel of the tiny car, she leaned down beneath the car top to say gaily, "I'm no longer sure what's etiquette in an office relationship and what isn't. Is it considered proper for a secretary to invite her boss to dinner?"

"I think it's highly proper, especially if the secretary is really a partner in the firm," Bob answered, obviously pleased. "I'll be happy to come to dinner. Like tonight, for instance?"

"If you are fond of fish," Donna told him, "then tonight would be fine. It's Mary's afternoon off and she's gone off somewhere to fish. So maybe you'd better make it tomorrow night! Come early, won't you?"

"The minute I shut the office, and I'll be looking forward to it," Bob said happily. "Remember me to Troy, will you?"

"Will do," Donna told him, and lifted her hand in a little gesture of leavetaking as she backed the car into the street and drove away.

"He's nice," said Gail happily.

"One of the best, and I'm shot with luck to be

able to work for him. He's going places, and has already made a good start. Who knows? Maybe he'll be Governor some day!" Donna said lightly.

"Or President?" Gail teased.

"After all, why not? He'd be a credit to the job." Donna laughed. "And now, on to the ice-cream."

Chapter Five

For the first few days, Gail felt a trifle shy with Troy, and then his unfailing courtesy, the fact that he seemed no longer to disapprove of her, erased the shyness and she began to feel at ease with him.

Donna had plunged into her job, and came home in the evenings filled with bright chatter about the day's happenings. She and Gail had become good friends at the very first, and now their friendship deepened, grew warm and strong.

Gradually, as the days slid past, Gail thought of Larry less and less often. He was part of the past that was tied up with Aunt Louisa, and neither of them was likely to intrude on her life again!

She had just gotten the children up from their nap one afternoon, and had them out in their sandpile, when she heard the clop-clop-clop of horse's hooves and looked up, startled, to see a girl riding down the shell-strewn drive. The girl's chestnut hair was almost the shade of the horse she rode, Indian-style, without a saddle. Her dungarees were crisp and clean, and her matching shirt was faded to a rich, deep blue.

Gail rose as the girl pulled up at the gate in the low wall about the patio and swung herself out of the saddle. She dropped the horse's reins carelessly and came swinging through the gate with a long-legged, easy stride that was at once graceful and somewhat studied. Her eyes were a cool gray-green, and they swept Gail from head to foot with a glance that was not exactly hostile but was certainly neither warm nor friendly.

"You're Gail Harrison, of course," was her brusque greeting.

"Of course." Gail smiled politely. "And you're Ellen Matthews."

The girl's airy brows went up slightly.

"Oh, then you've heard of me," she drawled.

"Why, yes, Donna mentioned you when I first arrived."

For a moment the two girls eyed each other appraisingly.

"I'll bet she did," Ellen drawled after that silent, intent scrutiny. "I hear she's gone back to work and dumped the kids on you, her nursemaid."

Gail smiled faintly. "If you think that's a phrase that hurts my feelings, Miss Matthews, you're very much mistaken. I love being a nursemaid to such adorable children. I've never been anything but a nursemaid, first to my elderly aunt and now to the children. It's a lot more fun being their nursemaid than being hers!"

Ellen looked without favor at the two children playing absorbedly in the sand, and then she dropped, uninvited, into a lounge chair and studied Gail intently, as she lit a cigarette without offering one to Gail.

Gail, determined not to be disturbed by the girl's frank animosity, merely waited, her hands in the pockets of her gingham play-skirt.

"I'm not a bit sure I like having you here," Ellen said at last.

"Oh?" Gail's tone was cool, polite, faintly surprised.

"Meaning there's not much I can do about it, of course," Ellen drawled.

Gail dropped into a wicker chair, and crossed her sun-tanned knees.

"Well, if Donna wants me here, and Troy is willing for me to stay—" she began.

"Willing?" Ellen caught the word and threw it back at her.

"Well, yes, of course," Gail answered. "This is Troy's home and, naturally, I wouldn't have stayed if he hadn't been willing to have me here."

Ellen pitched her cigarette into the brilliantly blooming pink begonias that bordered the sundial in the center of the patio and shrugged.

"Oh, well, so long as he is only willing, not eager—" she began arrogantly. Then she added swiftly, "Why did you come to Grove City, Gail?"

Gail stiffened. So it was going to be a battle, was it? All right! She'd give as good as was sent her way.

"I'm afraid, Miss Matthews, that's really none of your business," she said, coolly pleasant.

Ellen jerked up from her lounging position and stared at Gail, her eyes a frosty gray now, her mouth a thin, ugly line.

"Why, you little snip!" she gasped, outraged.

"I'm sorry you feel that way, Miss Matthews," Gail said dryly. "But, after all, I really can't see why you should be so upset at my being here. As long as Donna needs me and Troy is willing—"

"I have plans for Troy," Ellen announced flatly.

"Have you now?" mocked Gail sweetly. "Does he know?"

The color deepened in Ellen's face and her eyes were bright sparks of outrage.

"That is none of *your* business," she snapped.

Gail shook her head, smiling faintly. "I don't want it to be," she answered quietly. "What your plans are for Troy, what his plans are for you or anybody else, is most definitely none of my busi-

66

ness. And that's just dandy with me. My plans are simply to look after the children as long as Donna wants me to. Troy doesn't enter into any of my plans for the future."

Ellen studied her so sharply, so intently that Gail could only wait and wonder what was passing through Ellen's mind.

"I'd like to believe that," Ellen said slowly after a long moment.

"I truly wish you would, Miss Matthews," Gail said with such utter sincerity that Ellen was unwillingly convinced.

She sat twisting the cigarette she had not yet lighted, her eyes on the slender white tube. When she looked up at Gail there was a look of such utter sadness on her face that Gail was deeply touched.

"I suppose you think I'm an utter fool to come here like this and make such a scene," she said huskily at last.

"Well, since you seem to feel that I'm a danger to your plans, I'd say you have a perfect right to lay your cards on the table and insist that I do the same," Gail said with a quiet reasonableness that made Ellen draw a deep breath.

"I can't remember," Ellen said after another long silence, "when I haven't been in love with Troy."

Gail waited, watching her, feeling a deep sympathy for her.

"He was busy then getting himself established here," Ellen went on after another long moment of silence. "And there was my mother. Dad had sunk every dime we owned, and a lot we didn't own, into this fishing camp. It was mortgaged to the last boat; and we never seemed to reach a place where I could let go. After Mother died, and the fishing camp began to pay off, and Troy got on his feet financially—there was Donna and the two children for him to take care of. And my dad was always busy trying to 'rustle up a fast buck' and getting himself into trouble with the authorities and by the narrowest possible squeak managing to stay out of jail."

"I'm sorry," said Gail when Ellen fell silent.

Ellen looked up at her.

"So you can see," she said evenly, "why, when Johnny Osceola told me that you were here, I was —well, upset is scarcely the word. But it will have to do. And so I had to come and see for myself what you were like."

Gail smiled at her. "And now that you have seen, I'm sure you won't worry any more. No man in love with you would ever give me a second glance."

Ellen's face twisted in a brief, painful smile that was without mirth.

"Now that I've seen you, I'm more worried than ever," she admitted. "Because, you see, Troy is not the least bit in love with me."

"Oh, but Donna said—" Gail tried to check the words, but it was too late. Ellen tensed slightly.

"Well, go on. What did Donna say?" she demanded.

"Only that you and Troy were close friends, that you'd been going together for a long time but there had been—well, complications. And one reason she was so anxious to get back to work to support herself and the children was so she could remove some of the complications. I suppose she thought that you two wanted to be married."

Ellen had listened tensely, her slender, superbly moulded body taut. And then some of the tension went out of her and she relaxed, throwing away the shredded cigarette as if she couldn't remember what she had planned to do with it.

"Oh, yes, Donna thought Troy wanted to marry me. Unfortunately, the thought has never occurred to Troy!" She leaned forward suddenly, her face hidden behind her hands, and there was a faint quiver of her shoulders before she regained her control and sat up again.

She looked at Gail with eyes that were touched with shame.

"Sorry," she said huskily. "That was unforgivable of me. But if you could only know, Gail, what a horror it is to be deeply in love with someone who regards you as a sister, no more. But of course you couldn't know about that—could you?"

Gail's smile was thin.

"I'm afraid not," she admitted. For while she knew very well what it was like to be in love, it had not been with someone who looked on her as a sister. Larry looked on her as a first-class pest who didn't know the first thing about flirtation, and who took a man seriously when he was only pretending to be in love.

"Well, be darned glad," said Ellen. "It's a little less than no fun at all, I can tell you."

"I'm sure it must be," said Gail quietly.

Ellen stared off across the low patio wall to the jungle growth beyond.

"Well, I've been a first class fool to come here and act up like this. I suppose, when you tell Donna and Troy what an idiot I've been—"

Gail stared at her, shocked.

"Why, Ellen, you surely don't think I'd repeat anything you've said to them or to anybody else?" she protested swiftly.

Ellen stared at her, wanting to believe her, yet not quite daring to.

"You're not going to tell them?" she asked huskily.

"Well, of course not," Gail answered. "Why should I? It was strictly between you and me, so why not keep it that way?"

A look of such intense relief touched Ellen's face that Gail was embarrassed and deeply touched.

"I don't quite know how to thank you," said Ellen awkwardly. "I should never have come here, I know. I certainly should never have flipped as I have. But the moment I saw you and remembered what Johnny Osceola said about your staying here, I felt I had to see you."

"Who's Johnny Osceola?" asked Gail.

"Oh, he's Mary's nephew," Ellen answered, and this time she lit a cigarette and drew deeply on it. "Dad says he's the finest fishing guide in the Glades, and uses him as often as he can. I think Johnny's a poacher and so do most of the Park Rangers. But they like Dad and try not to get too tough with either Dad or Johnny. But one of these days they are going to catch Johnny redhanded and then he'll go to prison; and unless Dad watches his step pretty closely, he may go, too. The law is very strict about poaching, and the sentences handed out are severe. Of course, Johnny's tribe would do everything they could to help him; not to set him free, but in order to punish him themselves. If the government catches him, he'll go to prison. If the Seminoles catch him, he'll be exiled for as long as they think best."

Gail said, wide-eyed, "Exiled where, for goodness sake?"

Ellen shrugged carelessly. "Oh, there are miles and miles of the Glades known only to the Seminoles. And when they convict a member of the tribe of a crime, they simply order him into the interior and forbid any of the tribe to speak to him. He is strictly on his own. If he starves to death, or is bitten by a poisonous reptile, or falls afoul of a dangerous alligator—well, that's too bad, but it is undoubtedly the work of the Great Spirit, who agreed that his crime was punishable by death."

Gail drew a deep breath. "And if this Johnny Osceola is caught poaching, they'll do that to him?"

"If they can convict him before the Rangers catch him!" Ellen agreed, and looked faintly amused. "After all, Gail, it is their ancient tribal custom and we have no right to interfere. Uncle Sam leans over backward not to interfere in their rites and customs. He's there to help if they want him too. But otherwise, the law of the Glades is—hands off!"

Gail looked out across the creeping jungle and shuddered.

"And any man, Seminole or white, would risk that for just a few dollars?" she asked uneasily.

Ellen shrugged and scrubbed out her cigarette in the gravel that covered the path at her feet.

"Oh, it's not the money that appeals to Johnny," she said carelessly. "The white traders he has to deal with cheat him and rob him, and he knows it. He can't dispose of what he poaches, so he has to turn it over to them. And he makes much more money conducting fishing trips. It's simply, I think, the feeling that since he is a Seminole and this is the ancient Seminole country, the government of the United States has no right to deny him the privilege of doing anything he wants to do!"

She stood up suddenly and glanced at the watch on her wrist.

"I'd better be getting back to Ibis Camp," she said. "Dad and Johnny both have groups out fishing, and they'll come in starved. If I'm not there the cooks won't have supper ready."

Gail walked with her to the low gate in the patio wall, where Ellen paused and looked down at her from the saddle.

"You're quite a gal, Gail. If I must lose Troy to some other gal, I suppose I'd rather it was you," she said. And without waiting for Gail to answer, she picked up the reins, thrust a heel against her horse's flank and went swiftly down the drive and into the road.

Gail watched until the big chestnut had galloped out of sight before she turned and went back to the children. But as she amused them throughout the afternoon, she could not get Ellen out of her mind.

Donna's little car came racing up the drive and flashed into the carport, with Troy only a few yards behind her. Troy got out of his car and stood for a moment looking sternly down at Donna.

"One of these days, that kiddy car of yours is going to up-end on a curve and we're not going to be able to find enough of you to make a decent funeral," he told her sharply.

Donna put out a placating hand, all remorseful smiles.

"Was I driving too fast?" she asked sweetly.

"You were just flying low, that's all. You scare the daylights out of me!" Troy scolded her.

"I'm sorry, honey! I was just so anxious to get home to the babes." Donna's tone was warmly conciliatory.

"Well, if you don't stop trying to race like a fool, you'll be a long time getting home to them," Troy told her and stalked into the house.

Donna came through the patio gate, grinning impishly at Gail.

"He's mad at me!" she confided unnecessarily, and bent to scoop Cissy up into her arms. "Did booful baby miss ums muzzer?" she cooed, and Gail grinned, knowing that Troy's lecture had slid off Donna like water.

"Donna, you really should listen to Troy," Gail protested.

"Were they angels, Gail?" asked Donna, Troy's warning already forgotten.

"They were not, and you darned well know it." Gail laughed. "They quarreled and fought like the cats of Kilkenny. Wasn't that what you expected?"

Holding Cissy, Donna looked up anxiously at Gail.

"You're not going to walk out on them, and me?" she pleaded.

"Don't be a goop! If they were angels, Donna, they wouldn't be normal children! They're healthy and sturdy and very rugged little individualists, and I love them! And looking after them, after running errands for Aunt Louisa, is a breeze. Come on, Buddy, m' lad, bath time and then supper time and then beddie-bye!"

She lifted Buddy, who roared with fury as always. And with Donna bringing Cissy, they moved into the house and to the nursery.

Chapter Six

When the children had been put to bed, and Gail had showered and changed into a cool thin dress for dinner, she found Donna and Troy in the big living room waiting for her. By now, Troy had discovered that she preferred tomato juice to a cocktail, and it was waiting for her in a thin, crystal goblet, with a slice of lemon beside it and a very salty cracker.

"I hear you had a caller this afternoon," said Troy.

Gail all but choked on her tomato juice and stared at him, round-eyed.

"But how could you possibly know that?" she gasped.

Donna was looking from one to the other, puzzled.

"Who was it, Gail?" she asked curiously.

"Ellen Matthews," Gail answered, and Troy grinned at her. "I suppose Mary told you?"

Troy nodded, his grin deepening, and Donna cut in crisply, "Always be quite sure that when anything happens here, Mary runs to Troy with the news. Espionage, I call it."

"I'm glad Ellen called," said Troy pleasantly. "I'd been meaning to take you to Ibis Camp to meet her and her father on my first free weekend, but there has been something to prevent that each weekend since you have been here. What did you think of her?"

Gail looked down at her tomato juice, squeezed a bit more lemon into it, and tried to remember that Ellen had broken down and confessed her love for Troy.

"Why, I thought she was lovely. What else could I think?" she answered awkwardly.

Troy's brows drew together in a small, puzzled frown.

"Lovely? I'd never thought of Ellen as lovely," he said slowly. "She's a wonderful person. And the way she has pulled Ibis Camp together and made a success of it is almost miraculous. But lovely?"

"Beauty," stated Donna flatly, her eyes merry at the cliché, "is in the eye of the beholder!"

"You don't say!" Troy's brows went up in elaborate surprise, and then he grinned. "Oh, well, I suppose I've known Ellen so long I'm too accustomed to her as a person ever to think much about what she looks like."

"Why!" gasped Donna, outraged, "you dirty dog! That's an unforgivable thing to say about any woman! You should have your mouth washed out with soap and water."

"Oh, simmer down," Troy urged her, laughing. "I meant no disrespect to Ellen. I admire her enormously, not for her looks, but for what she is: a darned fine girl and a very good friend."

And Gail, remembering Ellen's despair that afternoon, felt a deep stab of pity for the girl.

Mary's announcement that dinner was ready came before Gail had to make an answer.

When they were at the table, Donna said briskly, "I'm going to be home this weekend, Troy. Why don't you take Gail out and show her the sights?"

"Oh, that won't be necessary," Gail said hurriedly.

"It might be fun, though." Troy smiled at her. "I have to go over to *La Casa Mañana* in the morning, Saturday. The pickers will be in the groves Monday and I have to see that things are ready for them. Would you like to go, Gail?"

For a moment Gail was still. *La Casa Mañana* was the Stillman home.

Donna said swiftly, "Of course she doesn't want to go there, Troy!"

Gail said, chin tilted, "Why not? I'd love to see the place."

Donna studied her for a moment, and then she grinned and relaxed.

"Well, it might be fun, at that. The greenhouses are marvelous, and Murchison would love showing you the orchid collection. I understand it's one of the finest in the country," she agreed briskly. "There are a lot of other things you should see there, too, I have no doubt."

Gail spoke to Troy. "Are you sure it wouldn't be a bother to have me along?"

"Of course not," Troy answered her so promptly that she was convinced he really meant it. "I'll leave you in Murchison's hands, while I make sure everything is ready for the pickers. And then we'll see what turns up later."

"Sounds like a lot of fun, and I'd love to go," Gail answered.

"Good! Then I'll ride herd on the babes!" said Donna happily. "I don't want them to forget me."

"Small chance of that!" Gail laughed. "They can't wait for you to get home in the afternoons."

Donna beamed, went on to an amusing anecdote about her day in town, and the evening progressed on its usual way.

Saturday morning, Gail climbed into the station wagon with Troy and waved goodbye to the children, who were none too pleased to see her go.

"I do hope you don't mind my being along,"

Gail said shyly as Troy eased the car from the driveway into the highway.

"I wouldn't have asked you if I had, would I?" he pointed out.

"Well, you didn't really ask me," Gail reminded him. "Donna practically forced me on you."

"Oh, no, she didn't!" Troy insisted firmly. "Donna may try, but she does not get her own way by trying to force me to do anything. I don't allow it!"

Gail's eyes danced a little, but demurely, she said nothing. If he thought that, why disturb his complacence?

"Matter of fact, I'm beginning to wonder if some of the excitement of Donna's job may not be wearing a bit thin," Troy said as the station wagon sped along the road. "She misses the children, but she doesn't want to admit it, now that Bob is tickled silly to have her with him."

A small, taut uneasiness settled in Gail's heart. Was Troy right? Was Donna already regretting that she had turned the children over to her, Gail? And would Donna give up her job and stay home with the children? And if she did, what would Gail do?

"Well, here we are," said Troy, his voice breaking into her thoughts as he turned the car from the highway through tall iron gates set in a six-foot wall of cream-colored stucco that was splashed with bougainvillea.

Troy brought the car to a halt and sat for a moment looking down into Gail's face. He said very quietly, "Yes, this is Larry's home. One of them, anyway."

"It's beautiful," Gail said. "But it scares me."

Puzzled, Troy asked, "Scares you? Why should it?"

"Well, if Larry *had* wanted to marry me, and *had* been waiting for me at the bus station, I might have had to live here," she burst out with such unexpected candor that Troy could only stare at her. "And I'd have been terrified. Why, there must be dozens of servants to manage—and a lovely house like this—Oh, no, I like *La Casita* much better!"

Troy stared at her for a moment, and then suddenly he laughed.

"You really are an amazing creature, Gail. I thought managing dozens of servants and a huge establishment like this was what every girl in her right mind yearned for!"

Gail's color deepened.

"Then maybe I'm not in my right mind," she admitted. "There have been times since I came to Florida when I've been willing to admit that."

"Then you no longer feel so badly about Larry's run-out?" he asked.

Her mouth tightened a little but she kept her head high.

"I don't blame him a bit. I'm the one to blame for being such a fool, taking so much for granted," she confessed frankly. "And I won't ever be able to thank you and Donna enough for taking me in as you have. I'll be grateful as long as I live!"

"There's no need for you to be all that grateful, Gail," Troy told her. "I think you can see what your being here has done for Donna. She is tickled with her job, and knows that her babies are cared for properly."

"They are such darlings!"

"They are, aren't they?" Troy agreed almost in the tone of a proud father, then laughed at himself. "It's meant a lot to me having them here, I can tell you. I'd been sliding along alone, feeling pretty self-sufficient, quite sure that I was completely contented at *La Casita*—until they came. Then I realized that I'd been damnably lonely but too stubborn to admit it."

"You're sure you don't mind me being there, too?" The words came from Gail involuntarily, and she could not have stopped then, even if she had realized in time how revealing of her inner emotions they were.

Troy turned and studied her for a moment, his eyes taking her in, lingering a little on the softness of her mouth, before he gave her a smile that startled her by its warmth.

"Quite sure," was all he said. But the tone and the look added its own special emphasis that brought the color in a warm tide to her face.

A man who came along the path from the

groves hailed them, and Troy got out of the car and went to meet him. They shook hands, chatted for a moment, and then the man nodded and went back along the path.

Troy came back to the car and opened the door for Gail.

"Murchison's in the potting shed," he explained. "I'll have him show you the orchids while I check with the grove superintendent. And then we'll go somewhere for lunch."

"If you're sure you have time?" Gail hesitated.

"I have time," said Troy, and chuckled, though at what she couldn't be quite sure.

They went along the path, back of the big garage. There, sheltered by the bulk of the garage and service quarters, was an enormous greenhouse, some of its windows elevated slightly, some of them painted white to soften the sun's rays.

Troy walked to a door at the far end of the greenhouse and tapped against the glass panel. Through the windows Gail could see a stout, middle-aged man in working clothes come along an aisle between rows of shelves that held a huge number of small flower pots, each one holding a small, brave sprig of green.

The man opened the door to Troy and Gail, and beamed at Troy.

"Well, hi, Troy, glad to see you," he said, wiping his earth-stained hands on a filthy old rag as his eyes went with lively interest to Gail.

"Brought a friend to see your orchids, Murch," said Troy. "Gail, this is Murchison, one of the finest orchid growers in the whole United States. Murch, this is Miss Harrison, a guest at *La Casita*."

"What do you mean, one of the best?" protested Murchison, and turned to Gail. "Like orchids, do you?" he asked.

Gail smiled into his twinkling eyes and answered frankly, "I'm sure I do, though I've never seen any."

"Zounds, girl!" Murchison was horrified. "Where have you been living, for Pete's sake? In a cave?"

"In a small town in Kentucky, where we run mostly to Grand Duke Cape jessamine instead of orchids," Gail laughed.

"Grand Duke Cape jessamine, eh? Gardenias, we call them," said Murchison, amused.

"I'll be back later, Gail," Troy told her. And to Murchison, "I want to check on the arrangements for the pickers next week, Murch. The crop looks good, doesn't it?"

He nodded to both of them and, without waiting for Murchison's answer, turned and strode away. Murchison watched him for a moment and then turned to Gail with a friendly, twinkling smile.

"Well, come along and let me show you my babies," he suggested, and held the door open, closing it behind her as she walked into a heat that made her catch her breath, so humid and heavily odorous was it. "I have to keep the temperature pretty high in here until the cuttings are rooted. Can't afford to ship any that aren't sure to grow."

Gail walked along the narrow plank walk between the rows. At the far end, Murchison opened a door, motioned her through it and once more closed the door swiftly behind him. The shelves, like those in the potting shed, held a vast number of small pots; but in these pots the plants were larger, healthier-looking, and here and there one showed the swelling of a bud.

"The result of seven years," Murchison told her, as he paused to indicate one of these. "Imagine waiting seven years for something like that and then having some purse-proud female pin it on her dance frock to die in a single night!"

"That seems wicked," Gail admitted frankly.

Murchison shrugged lightly, his thick shoulders rising as he grinned at her.

"Oh, well, if no female wanted to wear one, I wouldn't be in business," he chuckled. "After all, it's the florists who buy them, and the plants back there barely manage to keep a fellow in business."

Another door opened and swiftly closed, and they were in the section from which Murchison made his shipments of blossoms. Gail caught her breath and stood enchanted. For here all the pots held blossoms ready for cutting, and she had never dreamed there could be anything so lovely. The delicate things were like a flight of exquisitely tinted butterflies, and she stood above them while Murchison watched her, pleased because she was so obviously all but worshipping the fragile, exquisite things to which he had given so much of his life.

"Like them, do you?" he asked at last.

"*Like* them? Oh, I never dreamed there could be anything so beautiful!"

Murchison nodded. "Then I'll show you my finest ones, in the place where I take people who aren't quite sure they want to grow orchids until I show them what can be done with them. And that usually results in a very handsome sale of cuttings. Funny, they always seem to think they can grow them, once they've seen my beauties."

The door at the end of this room was painted white, and hid what lay behind it. Murchison opened the door and stood aside as Gail walked past him and stood breathless with delight.

It was a small room, but it had been lovingly decorated, turned into a sort of garden-room. Instead of shelves with rows and rows of plants, here the orchids were growing in large pots and baskets, their background an artfully contrived jungle of living green. In the back wall there was a small fountain: a lion's head spilling water into a series of graduated bowls until, at the bottom, a narrow, rock-bordered path carried the overflow out of sight. There was a mossy path here instead of the plank walk in the other rooms, and orchids grew along the branches of trees in a faithful imitation of their native state, the pots that held them concealed by green moss. A great splash of exquisite pale pink blooms, very tiny, swung downward from a basket attached to the back wall just above the small fountain.

"Oh, those are exquisite," gasped Gail, and Murchison chuckled.

"Oh, those," he said casually, yet delighted by her admiration, "are wild ones. I wangled a couple from one of the Park Rangers and tried hybridizing them. But they wouldn't mix with the tame ones, so I just let them grow as they wanted to."

"These came from the Everglades out there?" asked Gail, wide-eyed.

"Oh, there are about fifty varieties of wild orchids growing in the Glades." Murchison answered. "You must be sure to have Troy show you some of them. Of course, a lot of them grow in places inaccessible to anybody, even the Rangers. Which is as it should be. The Glades have a right to protect some of their wonders from prying eyes and pilfering fists!"

When they left the room, she noticed that he carefully locked the door and pocketed the key. As he saw her watching him, he grinned.

"Always keep it locked," he explained, "for fear I may forget sometime when Stillman's here and some of his fancy friends will get in and wreck the place. Of course, the whole business really belongs to him, and he gets all the profits. But I have had some rare old battles with him about my babies in there. He can turn his friends loose and let them chop the blooms everywhere else, but not in there."

Gail felt her face grow warm, but she only said lightly, "Is he here very often?"

"No, thank the powers that be," answered Murchison, and there was active dislike in his voice for the man who was his employer.

Gail looked over the pots of blooming beauties and sighed. "I can't imagine any woman cutting one of those lovely things just to wear for a single evening. I can't imagine Larry allowing her to."

Murchison looked at her sharply.

"Oh, do you know Stillman?" he asked, as though regretting his frankness.

Gail hesitated for just a moment, and then she smiled. "I've met him, but I don't really know him."

"Well, if you see him the next time he's around, I hope you'll forget anything unpleasant I may have said—" Murchison began awkwardly, and added quickly, "Not that I'd mind telling him myself. But if I did, he'd fire me, of course. And I couldn't abandon my work. I've put twenty years into it, and—well, it's the only work I really love."

"I doubt that I'll ever see Larry again, and if I

do, I surely won't be a tattletale," Gail assured him earnestly. "I'm on *your* side, Mr. Murchison!"

"Well, now, it's a relief to know that!" Murchison said frankly. He looked over the rows of plants and asked, "Which one would you like?"

Gail put out her hand swiftly to his and shook her head.

"Don't you dare cut one of those for me!" she protested.

"Who was going to cut one?" Murchison asked, frowning. "I was going to give you a plant, any one you like."

"Oh, no, thanks," Gail answered, and smiled warmly at him. "Just seeing them and remembering their beauty is enough. But it is kind of you, and I'm grateful for the thought."

Murchison smiled at her. "It's here for you any time you want it," he told her. "I heard Troy say you'd be going to lunch after you leave here, so maybe it would be better if you get it some other time. But be sure that it's yours, any time at all."

Gail thanked him warmly. As they came out through the potting rooms into the brilliant noonday sunlight beyond, Troy was coming up the path from the grove, walking with the man who had come to greet him earlier. For a moment they stood talking, and then Troy nodded, clapped the man on the shoulder, and came on to where Gail and Murchison were waiting. The other man went back toward the grove, and Troy smiled at Gail and Murchison.

"Crop looks fine, Murch," said Troy happily. "That's good, because the co-op is anxious to load two ships at Tampa in a couple of weeks. Looks like a good ten-to-twelve-thousand crop from here. Mine won't be ready for another couple of weeks."

"Well, the market will be good then, maybe even better than now," Murchison answered. "I've got quite a few orders for my babies to ship, so Stillman ought to have a nice little profit from *La Casa Mañana*—not that he needs it, of course. Still he'll want it, every blinking penny."

Troy looked swiftly at Gail and answered with careful lightness, "Well, after all, the place is his, Murch, even your beloved orchids. And a man has the right to what is his."

"Wouldn't you like to think what Stillman would have if he had to soil his pinkies by working at honest labor?" drawled Murchison. He looked swiftly at Gail and grinned ruefully. "You can forget I said that, too, the next time you see him."

Troy's expression sharpened, and Gail avoided his eyes as she said, "Oh, I doubt very much I'll ever see him again, Mr. Murchison. And as I said before, I'm no tattletale."

Murchison looked at Troy, then nodded toward Gail.

"She's a nice girl," he said.

"We think so at *La Casita*," Troy agreed. When he and Gail were in the station wagon, driving away from the big house, he asked her courteously, "What did he mean by saying 'the next time you see Larry?' Did you tell him how you happened to come here?"

Gail caught her breath as though he had slapped her.

"Do you really think I'd be such a fool?" she protested sharply. "He asked if I knew Larry. I said I'd met him but I didn't feel I knew him. He seemed pretty bitter about Larry wanting all the profits from the orchids, and told me he kept the door to what he called his private sanctum locked all the time so Larry's friends couldn't get in there and help themselves."

Troy nodded and gave her a relieved, apologetic smile.

"Sorry," he said quietly. "It's just that I didn't want anyone except Donna and myself to know about you and Larry. For your sake; not for his."

Gail said huskily, "Thanks. I'd much rather keep it that way, too."

She felt his eyes upon her for a moment, and would not meet them. And Troy, who seemed to understand her feeling, spoke casually of other things as the car reached the highway.

"And now let's see about some lunch, shall we?" he suggested, and slowed as he waited for her to answer. "Where shall we go? I'm afraid it's a little too far to Miami, but there are other places."

"Could we go to Ellen's place?" asked Gail.

"You mean Ibis Camp?"

"If that's Ellen's place. I like her."

"It's Saturday, and the place should be serving lunch," Troy agreed. "It's an interesting spot and very beautiful."

"And Ellen is an interesting girl and very beautiful," Gail added, laughing.

Troy grinned at her.

"I may have said it before, Gail, but it'll bear repeating," he stated. "You are a most remarkable girl. It's not every pretty girl who is willing to admit another girl is beautiful."

Gail laughed. "Oh, well, maybe you just haven't known my kind of girl," she pointed out saucily. "I couldn't deny that Ellen is beautiful even if I wanted to. I'd like to be friends with her—if she'll let me."

But the last words were spoken so softly that Troy did not catch them.

Chapter Seven

The highway curved, and then there was a hard-surfaced road leading south into the park area. This road went through what looked to Gail like a wide plain, until she realized that the tall, waving grass was growing out of water, not land, and she gasped.

Troy chuckled. "The Seminole call it Pa-Hay-O-Kee, River of Grass," he explained. "There's a park in Georgia the Indians called Okeefeenokee, Land of the Trembling Earth. Their names for places translate as much prettier than ours sometimes."

Gail had no comment to make as she watched the tall grass waving gently in the breeze. They crossed a narrow bridge, and ahead the road forked abruptly. Troy took the left fork, and Gail caught a glimpse of a bird carved from wood, painted white, and dangling in its wooden claws a narrow sign that read: "Ibis Camp; Two miles."

The trees began soon after that, and she saw great humps of land covered by saw-grass and palmetto, and tall trees rearing themselves proudly as though taking pride in their ability merely to find root space in such marshy, swampy land.

The road ended as abruptly as it had forked, and ahead there was the gleam of water dancing in the sunlight beyond a cleared space where a large building sat. The building was merely roofed, and its sides were screened, not walled. Through the screens, she could glimpse small tables and waitresses in green uniforms hurrying about. On either side of the building there were a few neat small rustic cabins. The parking area was well-filled with cars, and opposite the restaurant building, a narrow pier, with boats of varying sizes nuzzling against it, jutted out into the water.

Troy got out of the car and came around to open the door for Gail. She smiled as she stepped out, her eyes taking in with delight the scene about her. But before he could say anything, there was a joyous yell and Ellen, clad in jeans and a shirt, came running toward them.

"Troy, darling, am I glad to see you!" she gasped. She threw a very casual glance at Gail and said curtly, "Hello, Gail," then turned back to

Troy. "Johnny's guiding a fishing party and Dad's AWOL, as usual. There's something wrong with the Number Two boat, and it's been chartered for the afternoon. The party will arrive at any minute and if I can't get the boat working, I'll lose the fifty dollars they were going to pay me. And, Troy, you know I can't afford it. Be an angel and come and fix it for me."

Troy laughed. "Thanks for the compliment, Ellie!"

"Run on inside, Gail, and order. This shouldn't take long. You'll excuse me?"

"Of course," said Gail, and smiled at Ellen, whose brows drew together in a slight frown as Troy hesitated long enough to apologize.

Gail sat down on a bench at the end of the small point of land and looked about her. Behind the restaurant building, huge mangrove trees towered above a narrow brownish stream. But opposite the building, the pier jutted out into water that was free of the dark brown color and also of the jutting roots of trees. Obviously a channel had been cut here for the free passage of fishing boats.

From where she sat, Gail could see Troy and Ellie hovering above the engine of a smart, expensive-looking cabin cruiser.

She was startled by a pleasant voice that spoke behind her. A man had emerged from one of the neat rustic cabins and stood looking down at her with lively interest. He was a man perhaps fifty or a few years younger, well-built, not fat but solid-looking. His bare head was covered with a thick thatch of iron-gray hair that was crisp and inclined to curl. He was sun-bronzed almost to the color of the Seminoles, and he was clad in immaculate gray cotton trousers and a matching shirt, with a well-knotted and rather flamboyant tie beneath the buttoned-down edges of his collar.

"Well, well, well," he greeted Gail, "what have we here? Don't tell me you're going fishing in that pretty frock and high heels. And you're too late for the Boat-a-Cade. It took off before ten."

"I came to lunch with Mr. Benton," she explained politely.

"Oh, the faithful Troy, eh?" The man grinned and dropped his voice to a conspiratorial whisper. "I'm Jim Matthews, Ellen's old man. I always keep out of sight when there's trouble around here. I know that if Ellen can't cope, some besotted male will be along to put things right. No real sense in my getting dirty trying to do something I know to begin with that I can't handle. I don't know the first thing about motors. And d'you know something? I've no intention of learning, because then I'd be expected to do the many repair jobs that are always turning up."

Gail said impulsively, "Why, aren't you selfish? I think that's outrageous, to expect Ellen to do all the dirty work."

Jim's smile was not quite so warm, though he

wanted it to appear that he was completely undisturbed by her censure.

"But, my dear girl, Ellen's mechanically minded, which I am not," he purred sweetly. "And besides, Johnny Osceola is the camp mechanic. It was up to Ellen to have him check the Number Two boat before he left on his guiding trip."

Gail felt her color rise, but she managed to set her teeth hard against any attempted retort. Jim stood beside the bench, one foot resting on it, his eyes taking her in from head to foot.

"I somehow get the idea that Ellen has discussed me with you," he hazarded after a moment.

"I've only met Ellen once before today," said Gail briefly.

Jim grinned ruefully.

"That doesn't answer my question, but we'll let it drop for the moment," he said and added briskly, "You're a friend of Troy's, obviously. The girl who's visiting at *La Casita*. I think Johnny said you were Miss Gail Harrison."

"That's right," Gail answered. "I'm looking after Donna's babies, so she can work with Mr. Jordan as his executive assistant."

Jim's eyebrows went up.

"So you're not merely visiting there; you're working there," he said as though somehow he found the thought interesting.

Gail smiled at him sweetly. "That's right: I'm a nursemaid."

Jim studied her for a moment.

"Were there claws in that?" he asked mildly.

There was a sudden popping sound from the cruiser, and then the motor settled down to a pleasant, steady roaring. Troy and Ellen stood up, beaming at each other happily.

A long, expensive-looking car was sliding into the parking area, and four men got out, equipped and clad for fishing. Ellen went to meet them, gracious, friendly, completely unaware of the smudge of grease that darkened one cheek, her hands busy with a piece of filthy waste on which she was wiping the grease stains and oil.

"Everything set, Miss Matthews?" asked one of the men importantly.

"Everything is fine, Mr. Caldwell," Ellen answered briskly. "We've just checked the motor, filled the gas tank, and here comes Billy, the guide, and his assistant, Joe, who'll look after you. There's a picnic basket aboard and a thermos of coffee! Have fun and lots of luck!"

The four men beamed happily at her and went striding out to the waiting boat, laden with enough paraphernalia for a three-week cruise, at the very least.

When they were out of hearing, Troy grinned down at Ellen.

"I suppose they filed a trip plan with the Park authorities, so if they get lost we'll know approximately where to look for them." He laughed.

"Oh, I filed a trip plan for them this morning with Ranger Martin at the office in Flamingo," Ellen answered lightly. "And they couldn't get lost if they wanted to, not with Billy and Joe guiding them. Come on; let's have some lunch."

She turned toward the restaurant building and for the first time seemed to remember Gail. Troy walked on to where Gail still sat with Jim Matthews beside her. The greeting between the two men was friendly, even genial; then Troy turned swiftly to Gail.

"Hi, I thought I asked you to go on inside and have some lunch," he scolded her. "I'm sure you must be starving. I know I am."

"Oh, do come in," urged Ellen, and gave her father an unfriendly glance. "Unless, of course, you two have already had lunch."

"We haven't," protested Jim. "We were waiting for you two."

"I was wondering where you'd gone into hiding," said Ellen, tight-lipped. "I might have known that, wherever it was, there would be a pretty girl close around."

Though her voice tried to make it a light remark, the glance she gave Gail was tinged with deliberate malice, and Troy looked at her sharply before he held out his hand to Gail and drew her to her feet.

Ellen led the way, tossing her head so that the sun turned its warm, rich chestnut to pure gold.

Gail looked up at Troy and then at Jim, and there was a flood of color in her face as she walked between them up the steps and into the restaurant.

Jim guided them to a table in a corner, and Ellen came back from the kitchen. Somehow it happened that she and Troy were seated side by side, with Jim and Gail opposite them.

A copper-skinned waitress, her pale green uniform setting off her well-developed figure, her sleek black hair drawn into a tight knot at the back of her well-poised head, came to the table with a heavily laden tray and smiled shyly at Gail.

"Hello, Miss Harrison," she greeted Gail shyly.

"Why—hello," answered Gail, puzzled at being recognized. The girl laughed.

"Aunt Mary has been telling us about you, Miss Harrison," said the girl. "She likes you very much."

Gail's brows went up.

"Well, thanks for telling me; I'd never have suspected it otherwise," she answered.

"Oh, Aunt Mary is old-fashioned. She's not quite sure that white people are friends of our people," the girl answered and, having finished her task, smiled and went away.

"See?" Troy laughed at Gail's expression. "Mary's related to every man, woman and child in the whole tribe. There's a rumor that Chief Billy scarcely dares call the Tribal Council into session without Mary's permission."

"I suppose it was Mary who decided the Seminole children shouldn't go to school at Big Cypress with the Mexican children, then," said Jim.

"Oh? I hadn't heard that," answered Troy cautiously.

"I must admit that Chief Billy had a few good points," said Jim easily. "Claims he wants the tribe's children to speak English and to learn white people's ways, which he maintains they can't do in a school where most of the children speak Spanish."

"I don't think the Chief took into consideration a few much more important points, Jim." Troy spoke so firmly that Gail sensed he felt strongly on the matter. "The tomato farms lease land from the tribes for their farming; and since tomatoes grow best each year on new ground, they return the land after they've used it for one season and move on. The land is diked, fertilized and ready for planting in pasture. You and I both know that the tribes are now in the cattle business, running something like two thousand head belonging to thirty or more families, and that in the past five years, the tomato people have returned to the tribes more than three thousand acres. And there's another thirteen thousand acres, mostly in clover, that's been returned to them. Where do the Chief and his tribes get off, to bite the hands that have been so good to them?"

Jim shrugged and grinned.

"Count me out, Podner," he mocked. "I'm strictly neutral. Whether the little Seminoles speak English, Spanish or their own language means nothing to me."

The waitress spoke crisply. "It mean a great deal to us, Mr. Matthews. You white people have come into our land and taken what you wanted. We have to live under your laws and regulations. Isn't it only fair that we should learn in your own schools to speak the language and follow the customs you are forcing on us?"

They all looked up at her, startled, for they had not been aware of her approach. Jim looked away, and Ellen said curtly, "That will do, Lucy."

The girl eyed Jim for a moment, her gaze frankly hostile, and then she turned and went away, her head high.

"Darn it, Dad," said Ellen, her voice low-pitched, vibrant with anger, "must you do everything possible to make things harder for me? I don't expect you to do anything to make things easier; but you know how hard it is for me to get help here. The only people I can rely on are the Indians, yet you never hesitate to insult them or sneer at them. I suppose you'd like me to do all the cooking and wait on tables and clean the cabins, as well as tinker with the boats? You won't be satisfied until that happens, will you? And you're busy as blazes trying to make it happen."

Jim was scarlet with anger, his eyes blazing, as he thrust back his chair and stood up.

"In that case, I have an idea my absence would be much more appreciated than my presence, so I'll leave you nice people," he said through his teeth. "So long, Troy. Nice to have met you, Miss Harrison."

He turned and strode out, and the screen door slapped shut behind him. Ellen watched him go; when she turned to Troy and Gail her face was set and grim, pale behind her sun-bronze.

"Sorry, Troy, Gail," she apologized briefly. "Shall we forget it?"

"Of course, honey," said Troy gently, and smiled comfortingly at her. "It never happened. Now let's eat! This is a delicious lime pie. You must give Mary the recipe."

Ellen gave a little spurt of laughter that was feathered with a threat of hysteria.

"Troy, you darling goose! It is Mary's recipe. You probably have it twice a week and again on Sunday!" she said. "Are we going to the rodeo? Tell me about it."

Gail watched and listened and felt isolated and alone.

It was late afternoon when she and Troy left the camp. On the drive back to *La Casita*, Troy scowled silently ahead of him, keeping his eyes on the road, and Gail left him to what were obviously not very pleasant thoughts.

When they reached *La Casita,* Mary met them with the news that Donna and the children would not be home until after dinner. They'd gone to town to the movies.

"She'll keep 'em up way past their bedtime, and they'll get their stomachs upset with the stuff she buys for them; then they'll be sick. But can't nobody tell her anything," sniffed Mary disdainfully, and went back to the kitchen.

Gail looked up at Troy and said anxiously, "Do you think that maybe Donna's tired of having me here?"

Troy looked astounded.

"Why on earth would you think such a thing?" he protested.

"Well, lately she's insisted on bathing the children and giving them their supper and putting them to bed herself," Gail pointed out. "She seems almost jealous of me!"

"Oh, come now, Gail. It was her own idea, remember? She wanted to work with Bob, and she couldn't unless you stayed and looked after the children. How could she possibly be jealous?"

Gail hesitated for a long moment and then she said soberly, "In her place, I would be. I mean if the babies were mine, I wouldn't let anybody else so much as touch them."

"No, Gail, I don't believe you would," he said so gently that she looked up at him, startled. "Donna feels that she must support the children, which is pretty silly. I am proud and happy to look after their future. After all, why else am I beating my brains out to build up a substantial stake, if not to take care of someone I love? Donna is all the family I have, and the children are very dear to me. I didn't want her to go back to work, but she was set on it. And then when you agreed to take care of the children daytimes, it all seemed a perfect solution."

"But now that she's been away from them for a while, she misses them, and I have a hunch she will decide she'd rather be here with them than working on a job," Gail pointed out quietly. "And when that happens, there will be no further need for me."

Troy frowned at her. "You mean you'll leave?"

"But of course. What else could I do?"

Troy was silent for a long moment, and there was a troubled look in his eyes.

"Where would you go Gail?" he asked gently.

"Well, I've learned a good deal about taking care of children since I've been here. And I might be able to get a job somewhere else looking after other people's children. Mightn't I?" Her voice pleaded for his reassurance.

"I suppose so, Gail, only I don't somehow like to think of your leaving here," he said slowly, and his eyes widened slightly as though the words surprised him.

"I might even get a job with Ellen," said Gail

after a moment. "You heard her say how hard it was for her to get help."

"Wherever you go, Gail, it's not going to be a fishing camp, not even one as well-managed and as thoroughly respectable as Ibis Camp," Troy told her. "And anyway, aren't we jumping the gun a bit? Just because Donna had a sudden desire to be with the children for the day, that doesn't necessarily mean she would want to give up the job she seems crazy about."

"It's just that she's been so kind to me," Gail answered with painful honesty, and added swiftly, "And you have, too, of course."

Troy smiled at her.

"Being kind to you, Gail, is no chore at all. It might easily become habit-forming."

Gail met his friendly, warm smile, and turned away from him, oddly and absurdly disconcerted.

"I'd better freshen up for dinner," she told him, and went out of the room with the feeling that she was running away from something dangerous.

She had barely reached her door when there was the sound of a car in the drive, and a moment later a scream that could only mean that Buddy was not finding the world entirely to his liking. Cissy joined the chorus. And then Donna came in, carrying a struggling Cissy, with Bob Jordan behind her tending to Buddy, who was still howling.

At the sight of Gail, both children squirmed to

get down and ran to her. Gail bent, gathering them to her, and looked up at Donna, uneasy because of the way Donna was studying her.

"They're all yours, Gail," said Donna, with a false gaiety that did not reach to her eyes. "It's plain that they want you and not their mother."

"They're tired and fretful because they're sleepy," Gail said defensively.

"I'm sure," drawled Donna. And as Troy came to the living room door, she flung him a bright-eyed glance. "Bob and I are driving over to Miami to do a spot of pub crawling. Why don't you call Ellen and we'll make it a foursome?"

Troy lounged in the doorway, watching her as Gail drew the children toward the nursery.

"Ellen never dates Saturday nights, remember? Too much to do at the camp," Troy answered.

"Oh that's right, she doesn't! Poor Ellen! And Gail can't come with us because she has the babes on her hands," said Donna gaily, and smiled up at Bob. "So I suppose you'll just have to put up with me alone."

"That's a hardship?" asked Bob, and his tone was low and intimate.

Donna laughed, the soft, seductive laugh of a woman who knows herself to be desirable and admired.

"Give Bob a drink, Troy darling, while I go and change," she suggested, and went on to her own room.

Gail bathed the children and got them into bed, soothing their fretfulness, bending above them as sleep descended on them. When she straightened, Donna was in the doorway, watching her with a cool enigmatic look.

"Zip me up, Gail will you?" she murmured, and turned her back, settling the folds of her timeless black chiffon and lace evening gown about her beautifully rounded figure.

"Of course," said Gail, and attended to the small task. "You look lovely. That's a beautiful dress."

Donna touched the folds with disdainful fingers.

"It's an old rag," she said. "I've had it for ages. But the slip is new. You don't think lilac satin under black chiffon is too blatant?"

"I think it's very becoming, and you look stunning, and I do hope you'll have a lot of fun," Gail told her sincerely.

Donna hesitated, and said awkwardly, "I've simply got to go to Miami next Saturday and do some shopping. Sure you won't mind not having the day off? Because if I do, you'll have to stay and look after the babes."

"That's what I'm here for, isn't it?" asked Gail quietly.

Donna studied her for a moment, and a tinge of color crept into her face.

"Sorry you and Troy can't go with us tonight, Gail," she offered a tacit apology for her curtness.

"I had a lovely day today, Donna, and I'm not a very good dancer, and I'd really much rather stay here," Gail told her sincerely. "Isn't there some other girl you can get to date with Troy?"

Donna hesitated, and then she grinned impishly.

"You know something?" She bent forward, and her tone was conspiratorial. "I'd rather just date Bob alone. Isn't he a lamb?"

"He's very handsome and very nice," Gail agreed.

Donna nodded, smiling, turned on high spike heels and went swiftly along the hall to the living room where Troy and Bob were. A moment later, Gail heard them go out.

When Gail came back to the living room, Troy was waiting for her, and Mary had announced dinner. As Troy and Gail walked into the dining room, Troy said, holding Gail's chair, "Still think Donna is jealous of you?"

"I think she is, secretly, but doesn't want to admit it even to herself," Gail said frankly. "She's glad to be free to go out dancing, but she's terrified the babies will learn to love me better than they do her, which is just plain silly! They couldn't! She's their mother!"

And Troy, seeing the look in her eyes, forbore to answer.

Chapter Eight

It was late one afternoon, when Gail was deciding it was just about time to take the children in for supper and baths, that she heard a car coming into the driveway and looked up, with an eager smile that faded as she watched the tall young man getting out of the car and coming toward the low gate set in the patio wall.

For a stunned, incredulous moment she could only stare, quite certain that it couldn't be Larry Stillman! But it was, and he paused at the gate and studied her curiously, in her blue-checked gingham playsuit, her legs and arms tanned to a delicious toast-brown.

"Well, hello there," he said at last. He swung open the gate and came into the patio. "So you're still here."

Gail was unable to find her voice, and could only sit looking up at him, wide-eyed, shaken a little by the sight of him.

Larry studied her, and then he glanced at the children and back to her.

"I couldn't imagine why you hung on around here, and finally I came back to see," he explained casually, his hands sunk in the pockets of his very expensive and superbly tailored sports coat. "When Troy told me at *La Casa Mañana* this morning that you were working here as Donna's nursemaid, I felt I had to come and see for myself what had happened to you."

Gail said huskily, "I had no place to go, and Donna wanted someone to look after the children."

Larry nodded. "So Troy was telling me. I'd forgotten how pretty you are, Gail."

"Had you?" Gail's voice stuck in her throat.

Uninvited, Larry dropped into a chair across from her and went on studying her, his blue eyes warming a little as they crept over her.

"In fact," he admitted with a frankness she somehow found bitterly humiliating, "I'm afraid I'd forgotten just what you looked like. But now that I've discovered, I intend to stick around for a while."

"Do you?" asked Gail, and added deliberately, "Why?"

Larry laughed. "Oh, Troy seems to find you

enormously attractive, and I have great respect for Troy's judgment, so I thought it might be fun to find out just what you've done to the old boy. I've never known him to give any girl a second glance, except for Ellen Matthews. He's always been too busy to pay attention to women. Very dull-witted and short-sighted of him, I've tried to tell him, but he wouldn't listen. I've tried to point out to him that the greatest and most rewarding study of man is woman."

Gail felt a seething rage within her, and her voice came unstuck.

"And I'm sure you've given that study a lot of your time and thought," she said through her teeth.

"I have, indeed." He laughed, completely undisturbed by her rising anger. "And now I'm prepared to give it some more time and attention. I want to find out what there is about you that's jarred old Sober-Sides Troy out of his work-a-day life."

Gail rose, and her chin came up.

"I'm afraid you'll have to excuse me now," she said distantly. "It's time for the children's supper. I don't know when Troy will be back, but Donna should be here soon."

Larry grimaced, laughing. "Donna hates my insides," he mocked. "But I've been invited to dinner, so she'll have to put up with me, I'm afraid."

Gail asked swiftly, "Troy invited you to dinner?"

"Why not?" asked Larry coolly. "He works for me. He could hardly object to his employer dropping in for a meal, could he?"

"Troy merely manages properties for you because you won't stay here and do it yourself," Gail flung at him hotly.

"Troy manages properties for me and receives a hefty share of the profits, which he promptly plows into his own grove and cattle," Larry cut in, stung by her tone. "If I took the management of my properties away from him, he'd feel the bite, believe me!"

"I don't believe you!"

Larry studied her with an intentness that was insolent and deliberate.

"What's between you and Troy?" he demanded sharply.

"What a perfectly rotten thing to say, or even think," Gail blazed. "You ran away when you found I was coming down here to marry you."

"Well, natch." Larry seemed puzzled that this should have offended her. "What else could I do but take it on the lam?"

Gail said slowly, "You don't even deny it!"

There was such puzzlement in her tone that Larry's eyebrows went up.

"Well, why should I? It's the truth! Nobody could possibly be as simple-minded as you want me to believe you are. You were putting on a rush act just because I'd whispered a few sweet nothings in your ear, to kill some idle moments."

"Oh!" Gail gasped, writhing as though his words had been physical blows. "You—why, you're utterly loathsome!"

Larry got to his feet, his jaw set and hard, his eyes angry.

"Now wait a minute," he began hotly.

"No, *you* wait a minute," Gail flashed furiously. "When Troy tried to tell me why you ran away, I wouldn't believe it. I was such a simple-minded little fool that I believed in you—I thought you were wonderful! I all but broke my heart grieving for you after you'd gone. You *did* write to me, you know; you did write that you loved me."

"So what?" Larry answered grimly. "You kept smothering me with letters all tear-stained and bedazzled with romantic love language. I'd have been a cad not to have answered a few of them. You had told me you couldn't leave your old aunt, so I felt it was perfectly safe to write you. Who could dream that suddenly you'd kick over the traces and come racing down here?"

"Get out!" Gail ordered, her voice shaking. "Run away some more! Run fast and furious and don't ever look back!"

Larry laughed, and now there was admiration for her spirit in his eyes.

"Hi, the soft, furry little white kitten's got

claws!" he mocked her. "I like you a lot better, Gail, when you're spitting and clawing than when you're being all soft and cuddly."

Donna's car turned in the drive, and Gail bent and picked up the children and marched past Larry, her head held high. As she entered the house, she heard Donna's very cool greeting of Larry.

"So you're back, eh?" Donna' tone was frosty. "The bad penny always turns up, doesn't it?"

"So I've sometimes heard." Larry's tone was completely unruffled. "I was curious to know why the stray kitten was still here and thought I'd take a look."

Gail heard no more as she hurried into the house and into the nursery. Bright flags of color burned in her cheeks as she fed the children, gave them their baths and got them ready for bed.

Donna came in just as she was tucking Buddy beneath the light covers and Donna said softly, "It claims it was invited for dinner."

"So he told me," Gail answered grimly. "Would Mary mind if I had dinner in the kitchen with her?"

"Mary wouldn't, but I would," said Donna briskly. "Come on, honey. You're going to put on one of those trousseau frocks, and let me do your hair, and you're going to knock the creature's eyes out. I'd love to do that, by the way, with a nice forked stick!"

Gail gave a small, smothered chuckle.

"You sound gruesome!" she observed.

"I feel gruesome where that so-and-so is concerned," Donna said. "Come on. The babes are asleep, and I'll check on them now and then. But right now, we've got to get you all done up to the nines—or even the tens."

"But, Donna, I don't ever want to see him again!" Gail protested, even as Donna was drawing her firmly across the nursery and into her own room.

"Naughty, naughty, Gail! Hating the guy isn't the answer! Making him realize what he missed by taking a run-out powder will make him squirm a lot more. After all, he's been hated by experts, of whom I'm proud to be one."

"But he said that if he took the management of his properties away from Troy it could be very bad for Troy," stammered Gail.

"And you believed him?" Donna spoke over her shoulder as she went swiftly and deftly through the contents of Gail's modest wardrobe. "Haven't you learned yet you can't believe a word the creature says? If Troy refused to manage his properties any longer, the workmen on the place would steal him deaf, dumb and blind, and it would serve him jolly well right! Troy looks after the stuff for him simply because they went to college together. Troy does it as a favor. The share of the profits he gets are not worth all the time and trouble he gives. Oh, this is *it!*"

She held up a dress of chartreuse tulle, very airy and bouffant, the bodice snugly fitted and sprinkled with sequins.

"Come on, honey make it snappy. Mary will be wanting to serve dinner before you're ready," she urged.

Gail protested even while Donna was helping her into the fragile frock and spike-heeled silver slippers. But Donna did not even listen to the protests, and when at last she stood back and surveyed Gail, she nodded, laughing a little.

"And now let's see how old Runaway Larry likes what he ran away from this time," she crowed happily.

"Donna," Gail laid a hand on Donna's that would have urged her toward the door, "if you're trying to get me to snag Larry's interest and then laugh in his face—"

"Oh, for Pete's sake, honey, you've been seeing the Late, Late Show again! That's the oldest trick known to man or woman. No, I don't want you to flirt with Larry or make eyes at him or lure him so you can laugh in his face! I just want you to show him what a raving beauty you really are, so he can go off in a corner and gnash his teeth in rage that he missed you when he had the chance to grab you! Now, come on!"

As they went down the hall, they heard Larry's

arrogantly self-assured voice, the tinkle of ice in tall glasses. But when Donna and Gail appeared in the doorway, Larry became silent and stood up.

Larry's eyes swept Gail, from the top of her burnished hair swept artfully into a very sophisticated knot at the back of her proudly poised head to the tips of the silver slippers revealed by the uneven hem of her ballerina-length frock. And he whistled a low and very flattering wolf-whistle.

Gail's eyes went to Troy, who was staring at her as though he had never seen her before in all his life.

Donna said gaily, "Hadn't you better change, Troy, if you and Gail are going to get started right after dinner?"

Gail swung a frightened glance at Donna and then back at Troy, and said swiftly, "I'm sure you're much too tired to go out tonight."

Larry spoke instantly. "I'm sure you are, too, Troy old man. So why don't I take Gail to dinner and for whatever festivity she has in her mind?"

"I couldn't think of it," said Troy firmly, and put down his drink. "I'll be right with you, Gail honey, though it's going to be hard to make myself beautiful enough for anybody to look at *me* when I'm wearing *you* on my arm."

He smiled warmly at her and hurried out.

"Hi, what *is* all this?" demanded Larry peevishly. "I was invited here to dinner, and Troy said nothing about having a date."

"Should he have?" asked Donna with politely raised eyebrows.

Larry eyed her warily.

"Well, when a man invites you to dinner, you naturally take it for granted he's going to be there," he said unpleasantly.

Donna laughed lightly.

"Oh, we're going to feed you, Larry darling! Mary's cooking up a storm and I'm sure it will be delicious. But Gail and Troy have a date."

Larry looked down at Gail, then back at Donna.

"I'd like to talk to Gail, alone," he said firmly.

Donna raised her brows at Gail questioningly.

"Would you like him to talk to you alone, honey?" she asked.

"Well, of course she would," snapped Larry resenting the question.

Donna waited for Gail's answer, and Gail said huskily, "Well, after all, why not?"

Donna lifted her shoulders in a little shrug, and her smile was not quite so bright.

"As you say, after all, why not?" she agreed. "And anyway, I have to get dressed for *my* date. Bob will be here at any minute."

Larry waited until the brisk tapping of Donna's heels had died away, and then he looked down at Gail and there was a pleading look in his eyes that disturbed her for a moment.

"Look, darling, I know I don't deserve it, but

give me a break, please?" His tone was warm, intimate, almost caressing. "I admit I've been a first-class heel, but, darling, I didn't realize. Why, you've changed so that I hardly know you."

"If I have," said Gail, her voice low but her eyes meeting his steadily, "it's because Troy and Donna have been so kind to me. Away from Aunt Louisa, here in this beautiful country, I've been happier than I've ever dreamed I could possibly be."

"Happier even than when you and I were engaged?" asked Larry jealously.

Gail's smile was thin-lipped and cool.

"Happier even than when I *thought* we were engaged," she mocked him in an amused drawl. "I realize what a simple-minded fool I was to take you seriously even for a moment, Larry. Of course I never dreamed for a moment I'd be free to marry anybody. But then when Aunt Louisa suddenly decided to go abroad with her friends, I knew I was free to come down here to you."

A dark shamed color had touched his face, and his eyes could not quite meet hers.

She spread the skirts of her fragile frock and revolved slowly before him.

"Do you like my dress?" she asked him.

"Of course. It's lovely—you're lovely."

"It's one of my trousseau frocks," she told him in that gentle tone.

"A trousseau frock?" he repeated, faintly apprehensive.

Gail laughed softly. "Aunt Louisa gave me five hundred dollars and said that was all I could ever expect from her," she told him. "She said it would keep me while I was learning to do something that would help me earn a living. But I was so sure of you, Larry, that I spent every penny of it on a trousseau, and kept out just enough for bus fare and twenty dollars for food on the way down. Wasn't that idiotic of me?"

"Gail, I *am* sorry! I'm truly sorry! If you'll give me another chance—"

"So when I got off the bus, you weren't there, but Troy was." She seemed not to have heard him. "And then he told me that you got my telegram, but that you were scared and ran away."

Larry said harshly, "I didn't remember, Gail. I mean—well, if I'd had any idea what you were really like—"

"So Troy and Donna took me in and gave me a home, and I'm happier than I've ever been in my life, because for the first time I feel really secure."

"And just how secure are you here, Gail? What happens when Troy marries Ellen Matthews and brings her here to live? Then where will you be?" Larry demanded sharply.

For a moment a look of panic touched her eyes and she could not answer. Larry took a swift step toward her, caught her hands in his and lowered his voice to an urgent, intimate murmur, "Look, darling, I'm your very best bet for the future. Oh, I know you think you despise me now, but you don't. Not really, darling. You loved me back in Kentucky and I can make you love me again."

"So you can panic and run away again?" asked Gail huskily, shaken in spite of herself by his pleading voice, his hands that held hers so warmly.

"Darling-sweet, I'd never run away again!" he told her, his voice low and ardent. "I do love you, and I *do* want to marry you, just as soon as it can be arranged."

Wordless for a long moment, she could only stare up at him, tempted to believe him, yet knowing in her heart of hearts that she mustn't ever believe him again.

"Trust me, Gail darling, please?" Her hint of resistance, her hesitation fired his ardor even more. "I promise you, Gail you'll never again have any reason to doubt me! Just give me another chance, Gail sweet?"

What she might have said she would never know, for Troy was in the doorway, very striking-looking in his white dinner jacket. His eyes were on Larry's hands that held Gail's tightly.

"Sorry," said Troy briefly. "Perhaps I should have stumbled coming down the hall, or coughed to warn you."

Gail wrenched her hands free from Larry's

clasp and turned with swift relief to Troy, her eyes pleading with him to understand the situation he had disturbed.

"Ready, Gail?" Troy asked her, as Larry turned away, jamming his clenched fists into his pockets. "Or have you changed your mind?"

Gail looked up at him fearfully, for the tone was one he had not used to her since she had first arrived.

"Oh—no, Troy, no—that is, unless you have," she stammered.

"Sorry, Larry. I'm sure Donna and Bob will see to it that you have a nice dinner."

"Let Mary eat your dinner!" Larry snapped, and brushed past them and out of the house. A moment later they heard the sound of his car, shooting much too fast down the drive, tires screaming as he cut too short into the highway and roared off.

Gail said in deep relief, "Oh, now we don't have to go out to dinner."

Troy's eyebrows went up slightly and his eyes were cool.

"You find the thought so unpleasant? Having dinner with me, I mean, instead of Larry?" he drawled.

"Oh, my goodness, no! Troy, what a silly thing to say!" she stammered. "It was only that I knew you didn't expect to go out, and that you were tired, and Donna dreamed the whole thing up, pretended we had a date, just because she dislikes Larry so much."

"I don't dislike the guy," said Donna cheerfully as she came into the room, lovely in lounging pajamas of a green-blue shade that set off her lovely skin and eyes. "I purely despise his insides! I hope you gave him what he was asking for, Gail honey —a poke in the teeth and a kick in the pants. He's been asking for it, and it looks to me as if you might be the gal to give it to him."

Troy waited for Gail's answer.

"He said he was sorry and asked me to trust him and give him another chance." Gail's voice stumbled into silence at the look Donna gave her, and she didn't quite dare look at Troy.

Donna said after a moment, her voice odd and cool and difficult to analyze, "Oh, he did, did he? And what did you say?"

"I didn't say anything," Gail admitted. "I was too surprised."

"And that's when I came into the room and upset the proceedings," said Troy dryly. "Very inconsiderate of me. I apologize, Gail."

Gail flung out her hands in a little protesting gesture.

"Oh, please," she begged, "surely you know I wouldn't ever give him another chance to make a fool of me. Don't you think I have any pride, any self-respect at all?"

"Well, sure you have, honey," said Donna slowly, studing Gail intently. "But after all, he can be a darned persuasive guy, and he *is* quite a dreamboat—except that he always keeps sailing away at crucial moments."

Gail blinked hard against the tears that were threatening her.

"Don't you suppose I know that by now?" she asked painfully. "I can't ever be grateful enough to both of you for all your kindness and for all you've done for me! I never want to see him again, truly I don't!"

Donna nodded, her brows furrowed thoughtfully.

"What bugs the blazes out of me," she admitted at last, "is what the heck he's doing back here anyway."

There was a gleam of wintry amusement in Troy's eyes as he answered, "Well, don't let it bug you any longer. And by the way, that's an expression I'd never expect you to pick up working for a distinguished gent like Bob."

"Oh, Bob gets around among the younger set," Donna answered briskly. "There are a couple of typists in the office who are on the sunny side of twenty-five. And what did you mean, don't let it bug me?"

"Larry has come back because he was puzzled," stated Troy firmly.

"Puzzled?" Donna repeated. "About what? Or whom?"

"About why Gail is still here, of course," Troy answered. "I suppose he thought that the minute she found out he was gone, she'd climb back on her bus and take off for home."

"Because," said Gail with painful honesty, "he wouldn't have known I didn't have a home to go back to." She looked from Troy to Donna and finished huskily, "You see, he didn't dream that you two would take me in and make me welcome. And I suppose he's not very pleased that you did."

Before either Troy or Donna could speak, she went on, "He said he could make things pretty unpleasant for you, Troy, if he took the management of his properties away from you."

Troy stared at her, his brows going up until they threatened to reach his hair-line, and there was laughter in his eyes.

"Oh, come on now, Gail. Don't tell me he's twirling his black mustache and threatening to foreclose the mortgage on the old homestead unless you are nice to him! That's just a little too corny—even for Larry!" he protested.

Scarlet, Gail insisted, "But he did. He said it would take a large bite out of your income—"

"I told her the guy was talking through his toupee, Troy," Donna said briskly, and added eagerly, "Oh, there's Bob. You two had better get started if you plan to make Miami before all the pubs close."

Troy offered his arm to Gail as Donna went to

admit Bob. For a moment the four of them clustered in the hall near the front door, exchanging greetings, laughing. Then Troy and Gail walked out to his car, and Bob and Donna went to answer Mary's summons to dinner.

Chapter Nine

There was heavy traffic on the Tamiami Trail, and Gail sat beside Troy, saying nothing, as he gave his attention to the task of piloting the station wagon through the thick stream of cars and trucks.

She stole a glance at his rugged profile as he drove and felt a small stirring in her heart. He wasn't as good-looking as Larry, but he was very attractive indeed. And there was a small tremor of unhappiness as she recalled Larry's mention of Troy's marriage to Ellen.

"Cold?" Troy asked her, and she looked up at him, startled out of her thoughts. "You were shivering."

"Oh, no, I'm warm as can be," she assured him.

"It was just, as the Negroes sometimes say in Starkville, that 'a rabbit jumped over my grave.'"

"That sounds rather unpleasant." Troy smiled and then asked quickly, "See here, you're not taking anything Larry said seriously? I mean, about not letting me handle his property. I don't want you to believe for a moment that it would bother me in the slightest; in fact, it would really be a relief. I'd relinquish the whole business with great pleasure, believe me."

"I'm glad," said Gail eagerly. "I wouldn't do anything in the world that would cause you the slightest unpleasantness, after you have been so kind to me. I'll always be deeply grateful—no matter what happens."

Troy scowled above the wheel. "Now what's that supposed to mean—no matter what happens?"

"Well, you may not want me around much longer," Gail began awkwardly.

"Now where did you get that idea, for heaven's sake?"

"Well, from Larry."

"I'm beginning to believe he *is* raising big black mustachios to twirl when he meddles in other people's affairs," Troy said firmly. "Suppose we just forget about Larry for the evening, shall we?"

"Oh, let's!" she agreed so eagerly that Troy smiled warmly at her.

It was an evening she knew she would never

forget. There were the bright lights of Miami; the sweep of the causeway over which they drove to the Beach, passing the small islands with their brilliantly lit and luxurious homes; the unbelievable loveliness of Lincoln Road, with its lighted shop windows, its palms that stirred whisperingly in the soft air from the ocean, murmuring as it splashed in great rolling breakers on the golden sands; the night club where they dined on fabulous food that, for all that Gail knew, might have been ambrosia or sawdust. She was much too thrilled and happy to care.

When Troy asked if she would like to dance, she said with a humility he found deeply touching, "I'd love to, but I don't think I can. I've never tried."

"It's not difficult at all," Troy told her, smiling as he rose and drew her into his arms. "Just follow me—and the music, of course."

They made one circuit of the small floor, and she said, wide-eyed and delighted, "Why, I *am* dancing!"

"You're floating like a feather in the breeze." Troy laughed down at her. "You're a perfect partner."

She knew that wasn't true, but it made very pleasant listening.

When the evening was over and they were back at *La Casita*, he said, as he bade her good night,

"This has been a lot of fun. We must do it more often."

"Oh, yes!" she breathed ecstatically, then colored hotly as she met the look in his eyes. "I mean, any time Donna doesn't mind staying home with the babies, I'd love to go out with you, if you don't mind."

Troy said quietly, though there was a twinkle in his eyes that was amused yet warm, "I won't mind a bit. I'll be looking forward to it."

For a moment she had the utterly crazy, completely absurd idea that he was going to kiss her good night. And then he nodded, smiling, bade her good night and went on to his own room.

Lying in bed, feeling farther from sleep than she had ever felt in all her life, Gail went back over the evening. Her memories were so fresh and exciting that she was loath to exchange them for the uncertainty of dreams.

She had no idea how long she had lain there, halfway between happy walking and sleeping, when she heard the shrill clamor of the telephone. It was in the hall near the door of the nursery. Fearful lest the children be awakened, she slid out of bed and into her robe, hurrying out.

She lifted the telephone and said, "Hello?" softly.

A voice ragged, gasping, unrecognizable, said, "Gail? It's Ellen. Where's Troy? I've got to talk to him."

"Of course, Ellen. I'll call him," said Gail, and went swiftly to Troy's door and rapped softly.

His sleep-muffled voice called, "Yes?"

"Troy, it's Ellen. She's on the phone—she seems terribly upset," Gail told him through the closed door, and heard his swift footsteps as he came toward the door.

He emerged, belting his robe about him, and caught up the telephone receiver.

"Yes, Ellen, what's wrong?" she heard him say, and then saw shock registered on his face as he listened.

Donna's door opened and Donna stood there, startled and apprehensive.

"What?" Troy cried out sharply. "Pull yourself together, honey. Yes, I'll be there as fast as I can make it. Keep your chin up, darling. I'll be right there."

He put down the telephone and turned, scowling, to face Donna and Gail.

"Ellen's father is dead," he said starkly.

"Oh, no, Troy! How did it happen?" gasped Donna.

"He was shot," stated Troy in that same stark, shocked voice. "The police have been called. She's alone. I must get out there to her."

"Of course, Troy. I'll go with you," said Donna swiftly, and ran toward her own room, pausing at the door to say over her shoulder to Gail, "You aren't afraid to be left here with the children, Gail? Mary is here. You won't be alone."

"Of course I'm not afraid," Gail answered swiftly. "Hurry, Donna. Oh, poor Ellen!"

Donna hastily donned slacks and a shirt, and reached for a thin sweater. Troy came swiftly from his own room, hastily dressed in slacks and shirt, and went through to the carport as Donna finished her own sketchy dressing.

From the nursery came a child's whimpering call, and Gail sped to answer it. The noise had roused Buddy, who blinked at her in the dim night light as she switched it on and rubbed a chubby fist in his eyes.

"It's all right, Buddy, lamb," said Gail soothingly as she put her arms about him and gently pushed him back on his pillow. "Everything's all right. Gail's here. Go back to sleep."

Kneeling beside the small bed, her back to the door, she was unaware that Donna, hurrying out to the waiting car, paused for just a moment with a curious, enigmatic expression, a faint tightening of her pretty mouth. And then as Donna heard the sound of the car's motor starting up, she turned and went running out to Troy. A moment later the car left the driveway and Gail heard the sound of it dying away along the highway.

She soothed Buddy back to deep slumber, checked to see that Cissy was sleeping soundly, tucked the covers neatly over them and slipped out into the hall.

She caught her breath with a small, frightened gasp as a vast shadow loomed up before her, between her and the light from the living room. But almost instantly the shadow spoke, and she knew it was Mary, wrapped in a voluminous robe, tense and anxious.

"Where are they going at this time of night?" she asked of Gail.

"Ellen Matthews' father has been shot. He's dead! Ellen called Troy."

"Well, who else would she call?" Mary answered reasonably. "She's got no family to call on."

She was silent for a moment, and then she asked, "How was he shot? Why?"

"I don't know, Mary," Gail answered. "I answered the phone for fear it would awaken the children, and Ellen was hysterical. Troy came and talked to her, but she seemed not to be able to tell him quite what had happened, so he and Donna have gone to her."

Mary heaved a tremendous sigh.

"I've warned my nephew over and over again," she said half under her breath. "But being an Indian, and named Osceola, he still feels the great swamp belongs to the Seminoles, not to the white people."

Puzzled, Gail asked uneasily, "Mary, why do

you think your nephew is mixed up in Mr. Matthews' shooting?"

"They were poaching, of course, what else?" answered Mary grimly, her copper-skinned face dark with foreboding. "Probably it was for wild orchids. Johnny's too smart to bother with alligators or fancy birds. The white women won't buy egrets any more, and there's not much money in alligator hides. But wild orchids bring from twenty-five to fifty dollars a plant; and Johnny knows the exact location of forty varieties."

"And you think Mr. Matthews was helping him?" asked Gail uneasily.

Mary's eyes glittered in the faint yellow light that spilled out from the living room and reached the corner where they stood.

"I think Mr. Matthews has been urging Johnny on. It's Johnny's job to find the orchids, and that's no job at all; it's Mr. Matthews' job to contact the white traders and dispose of what Johnny brings him. It's Mr. Matthews who is at fault; not Johnny."

"And it's Mr. Matthews who is dead, Mary," said Gail quietly.

"And a good thing for Johnny and the other guides, too!" said Mary savagely, and strode away to her own quarters.

Gail went back to her own room, leaving the door into the nursery open, though quite sure now that the children would sleep until their usual waking time. She had no thought for bed. She curled up in a deep rattan chair beside the open window and watched the coming of dawn. . . .

The children woke, and summoned Gail back to her daily routine. She bathed them, dressed them for a morning in the patio sand pile, and gave them breakfast.

Mary, grim and worried, brought Gail's breakfast out to the patio and stood for a moment looking along the drive to the highway before she went back to the kitchen.

It was almost noon before Troy came back, and he was alone. He looked tired and grim, and Gail, seeing his haggard face, felt a stab of compunction at the thought that he had missed his night's sleep, so badly needed, more on her own account than on Ellen's. For it had been well past midnight when the Miami Beach date had ended and they had come home.

He smiled at her as he came through the patio gate, but it was a very faint, very tired smile.

"How is Ellen?" she asked at once.

"She's going to be all right," he answered, and dropped into a chair beside her. "It's been a terrific shock, of course. Donna is staying with her while I attend to some things in town. I had to come home and get into a somewhat more formal garb before I went into town. Lord, but I'm tired!"

He ran his hand over his haggard face, and

Mary appeared beside him with a tray on which were a pot of coffee, cup and saucer and silver.

Troy looked up at her and answered the question that was in her eyes and which she could not quite put into words.

"Johnny's not implicated in any way, Mary, so you can relax," he told her swiftly. "The police are convinced of that. It all started in a gambling joint somewhere. Jim got into a brawl with a couple of cardsharps, they fought, and later they tumbled his body out of their car at the Camp. After that, nobody knows where the men went, but the police have a good description of them and are quite sure they can pick them up eventually."

Gail saw the wave of relief that spread over Mary's face.

"It wasn't poaching, Troy?" asked Mary.

"It wasn't poaching, Mary, and Johnny has a perfect alibi. He was at a tribal conference the entire night. Chief Billy and half a dozen of the others will swear to that."

He smiled faintly at her and added with quiet emphasis, "This was a gambling scrap, Mary. No wild orchids were involved."

Mary drew a deep breath and nodded, turned and went back to the kitchen.

Gail poured coffee for Troy, and he thanked her, smiling as he accepted it.

"I'm ashamed that I kept you out so late last night," Gail said impulsively.

Troy managed a grin.

"Oh, did you keep me out late? I thought it was the other way around," he teased her.

"The whole evening was planned by Donna, just to make Larry jealous, and it was pretty silly," Gail insisted, very pink and very embarrassed, "as I should have realized from the very first. I guess I just let myself be carried away."

"And you don't think I enjoyed carrying you away?" Troy teased.

"I didn't mean it that way," protested Gail. "I meant that I shouldn't have let Donna persuade me to get all dressed up, and then when she told Larry you and I had a date, I should have said, 'Oh, no, we haven't. Troy's much too tired to go dancing.' That would have ended it, and you would have gotten a good night's sleep—at least until Ellen called you, and that was after three this morning."

"My dear girl," said Troy, and despite his weariness, he was grinning at her mockingly, "I enjoyed taking you dining and dancing a lot more than I would have enjoyed a night's sound sleep. So let's drop that argument. What I've got to do now is to get into town, see Bob Jordan and—well, make the arrangements for Ellen's father. We'll discuss our dating another time."

He put down the emptied coffee cup and scowled for a moment.

"The police are working on the case, but all

they know so far is that Jim was gambling with some men in a bar last night, and there were ugly accusations of cheating. The two men went out with Jim, still arguing and trading unpleasant epithets. That was shortly after midnight. A little after two, Ellen was awakened by the sound of a car outside the restaurant and went out to investigate. She found her father dead, and heard the sound of a car vanishing along the trail. It's hit her pretty hard. She and Jim had quarreled. You see, Ellen suspected he and Johnny were poaching wild orchids, and she knew that if they were caught, Jim would get a stiff prison sentence, and Johnny's tribe would drive him out. They have their own way of handling members of the tribe that disobey the white men's laws. Johnny was much more afraid of them than he was of the Rangers. And last night, they had him up before the Council. If he gets into any trouble at all just one more time, they'll give him a sentence a year or more alone: in a section of the Glades known only to themselves, where a man's chance of survival is very poor indeed. It's a sentence very much dreaded by all the Seminoles, so I don't think Mary need worry about Johnny any more. And I think the wild orchids are pretty safe, at least as far as Johnny is concerned."

He stood up, smiled at her and added, "Now I've got to get to town. Donna will stay with Ellen today and probably bring her home tonight. I'll see you at dinner time. Wish it could be a repetition of last night, but maybe some other time—"

She watched him as he went into the house, and her heart stirred a little, despite the situation that had developed. He had enjoyed last night with her. He hoped they would be able to repeat the evening's entertainment. And she hoped so, too, so ardently that she was faintly startled.

Chapter Ten

It was mid-afternoon when Mary summoned Gail to the telephone, and she heard Donna's voice, brisk and authoritative.

"Gail, honey, Ellen's decided not to come back to *La Casita* after all," Donna told her. "She feels she should stay here and see to things. Of course I don't want to leave her here alone, so I'm going to stay with her for a day or two. Is everything all right there?"

"Oh, yes, Donna," answered Gail. "The children are fine."

"Well, why not?" There was the faintest possible hint of dryness in her voice. "After all, Gail is with them, isn't she?"

Before Gail could answer that, Donna went on,

"I rushed off this morning clad in good intentions and very little else, and if I'm going to be here for a few days, I'll have to have some more clothes. So pack a suitcase for me, honey, and get Troy to bring it down here after dinner. The guides are all out with fishing and hunting parties. And Ellen's ready to fly apart at a second's notice, so I don't like to leave her. Anyway, her car has a flat tire, and I refuse to ride a horse home to pick up a suitcase."

"Well, I should think so." Gail laughed. "Tell me what you want, Donna, or do you just want me to use my own judgment about what to pack?"

"Oh, I think *I* can safely *do* that, honey. Just enough to tide me over for two or three days," answered Donna. "Of course, Ellen wouldn't be really alone if I came home, because the camp staff is here. But they are all Seminoles, and Ellen sort of clings to me. The camp is booked solid for the next ten days, and she feels she must keep things running. After all, this place is all she has in the world, and if she decides to sell it, she can get a better price if it's a going concern."

"Of course, Donna."

"Then you get Troy to bring me some things after dinner, will you, honey? And kiss the babes good night for Mommie, promise?"

"Well, of course I will, Donna. And give Ellen my sympathy."

"I'll do that little thing, Gail. 'Bye, now." And

there was the click of the receiver as Donna hung up the telephone.

Gail went into Donna's room, put a suitcase on a small stand beside the window from which she could watch the children, taking their afternoon nap on a blanket spread on the grass, and began packing. Her brow furrowed slightly as she sought among Donna's wardrobe for the things Donna would need for a few days at the Camp.

She put the packed suitcase beside the door and went back to the patio. The children awoke, dewy-eyed and filled with energy. She watched them lovingly, arbitrated when their squabbles grew too fierce, and eventually took them inside for their bath and supper.

As she tucked them into bed, she heard the sound of Troy's car in the drive and her heart leaped.

Then she heard footsteps in the hall and steadied herself, bending above Cissy, tucking the covers unnecessarily about the sleepy child. And then behind her a voice spoke, and she whirled to see Larry standing in the doorway, his eyes taking in the nursery, the drowsy children, and Gail busy getting them settled for the night.

"What a very pretty picture," Larry mocked. "So domestic! It makes me wonder if maybe I haven't been something of a fool."

Gail straightened and came across the room,

pushing him outside, drawing the door shut behind her.

"Larry, what are you doing here?" she demanded, her tone sharp, though her voice was lowered for fear of arousing the children just as they were slipping off to sleep.

"Now, I ask you, is that a friendly greeting? I come bearing a message from the master himself, my girl, and I'd thank you to keep a civil tongue in your head," said Larry, hurt.

"A message from Troy?" asked Gail, and caught her breath. "Something's happened to him? He's hurt?"

"Hey, you do fall apart at the thought, don't you?" Larry's eyes narrowed as he saw her swift, sudden pallor. "No, nothing's happened to old Troy. It's happened to the machinery at one of the packing plants, and Troy's Old Man Trouble-Shooter himself. All he has to do is walk into a room where machinery has been acting up, and it snaps to attention and goes busily back to work again."

"Oh, then he isn't coming home right away?" asked Gail.

"He doesn't expect to be here for several hours, and there wasn't time to call you. Matter of fact, he tried, but the line was busy," Larry explained. "So he called me and asked me to come over and explain. Afraid, I suppose, you'd be worried if he was late."

"I would have been," Gail admitted, her head high. "And besides, Donna is staying at Ibis Camp with Ellen and wanted Troy to bring her a suitcase with some clothes, as soon as he had dinner."

"Oh, then Ellen isn't here? Troy thought she would be," said Larry. "Suppose you and I drive down to the camp with Donna's suitcase?"

"Oh, but I can't leave the children," Gail protested. "And poor Troy has missed so much sleep and works so hard, I hate to think of him having to drive way down there after he gets home."

"Relax!" Larry urged, and his eyes were touched with resentment. "I said I'd run the case down, didn't I?"

"Oh, would you, Larry?" she asked gratefully. "It would be very kind of you. I'd appreciate it, and I know Donna and Troy would."

"Consider it done," said Larry briskly, and drew her with him toward the living room. "I'd do a whole lot more than that, Gail, if it would help me to square myself with you. Is there any hope of that?"

Gail looked up at him steadily.

"Of course, Larry. I'm really grateful to you," she said quietly.

Larry's eyes narrowed.

"Grateful?" he repeated. "I know I'm a fool to ask and I'll probably regret it—but what have you to be grateful to me for?"

"Oh, if you hadn't come to Starkville and let me

believe you were in love with me," Gail explained earnestly, "when Aunt Louisa decided to go to Europe with her friends, I wouldn't have known which way to go. But because you were here in Florida, I didn't hesitate. I just bought a trousseau and came rushing. And I met Donna and Troy, and they took me in. And I have you to thank for that."

Larry grimaced.

"I knew I'd be sorry I asked you," he admitted ruefully. "Well, now that Ellen is free to marry Troy, and Donna will eventually marry Bob, what are your plans for the future—or dare I ask that?"

"Oh, I've saved my salary that Donna has given me and I'll be just fine until I can find another job," she assured him sturdily.

"I'll bet you will, at that," said Larry slowly. "You're quite a girl, Gail, *quite* a girl!"

"Thank you," said Gail demurely, and a faint smile tugged at the vagrant dimple beside her mouth.

Larry was silent for a moment. He walked away from her, hands jammed into the pockets of his well-tailored sports jacket, and when he turned to study her, he looked very grave.

"I don't suppose there's any chance I could play any part in those future plans of yours?" he suggested at last.

Gail's smile deepened and a merry twinkle

touched her eyes and was gone before he could be quite sure he had seen it.

"Careful, Larry!" she mocked him. "You may have to make another run for it if you go around talking like that."

He was still studying her in frowning, deeply thoughtful concentration.

"Funny, but I seem to be getting the feeling that I've finished with running," he told her slowly. "At least from you, Gail."

"Oh, come now, Larry!" she mocked lightly.

"No, crazy as it sounds to you—and it sounds a bit insane to me, too, I admit— I have the most uneasy feeling that you and I could mean an awful lot to each other, given another chance," he said, and was so obviously deeply in earnest that Gail's smile faded and her eyes widened. "You loved me once, Gail. I *know* that. And you're not the kind of girl who can turn love on and off like an electric light switch. I believe, with all my heart, that if you'll give me and yourself another chance, something pretty wonderful might happen. How about it, darling?"

Gail said breathlessly, "Oh, now, Larry, you're taking an unfair advantage of me."

"An unfair advantage?" he repeated as though he had no idea what she was talking about.

"I'm still pretty unsophisticated, Larry, and maybe simple-minded enough to want to believe you—" she said. Her voice faded as he took a swift step toward her, and suddenly she was in his arms and his lips were on hers.

For a breathless, shaken moment that might have been moments or an hour, Gail neither knew nor cared, the kiss endured. When at last Larry raised his head a few inches and looked down at her flushed face, his eyes were brilliant.

"You see?" he told her huskily. "There's still a spark left! You haven't been able to get me out of your heart entirely, and it's only fair to warn you that I'm moving back inside! You're going to let me in, Gail, and we're going to be the two happiest people in the world. You wait and see!"

"Oh, Larry"—it was a small, frightened wail as she drew herself out of his arms and put her hands against his chest, pushing him away. "This is perfectly crazy!"

"Isn't it?" he agreed happily. "But it's also perfectly swell, isn't it? Gail darling, you can't deny that you returned my kiss, even that you liked it, can you?"

Gail put both shaking hands to her hot, flushed face, and there was a feather-edge of panic in her wide eyes as she looked up at him.

"Oh, Larry, Larry, why do you do this to me? I had gotten over you. I wasn't a bit in love with you any more. And now it's all starting up again." She turned from him as tears spilled down her face.

"You hadn't forgotten me, darling," Larry said

urgently, and there was triumph in his voice. "And I hadn't forgotten you. Oh, I tried to tell myself I had, but the moment I saw you here it all came back to me. Gail darling, you are going to marry me, and that's that."

And then he stiffened and his eyes went wide with shock.

"Did you hear what I said?" he asked, his tone low, fraught with the shock that registered in his eyes. "I asked you to marry me! I can't remember when I've ever said that to anyone before—they just sort of took it for granted—"

"The way I did, and then you had to run." Gail was recovering now from that moment in which she had given herself so breathlessly to the pressure of his arms about her, his kiss on her mouth.

"And wasn't I the prize fool?" he marveled, and reached for her again. But she evaded him and put a large chair between them, her hands flung up in protest.

"No, Larry, no," she said shakily. "You've got to give me time to think."

Larry leaned against the chair.

"There's been too darned much time for thinking, darling," he urged her. "Now's the time for action. Come on; let's go get married."

The world seemed to hang in the air between them for a breathless instant, and once again his eyes and his voice registered shock.

"I said it again!" he marveled. "And it's the

darnedest thing, but the more I say it, the more I really mean it! Can you imagine that?"

Gail's laugh was small and smothered, but she still evaded him as he would have reached out and gathered her close.

"No, I can't imagine it," she told him with a firmness that did not quite come off. "And you'll panic the minute you realize that you've said it."

"Maybe," he agreed cautiously and grinned at her, a grin that made her heart do a crazy kind of nip-up. "I don't believe I will! But if I do, you stick with me, darling. It'll be just a short panic, and I won't get farther than Miami. Promise you'll run me down?"

"I promise nothing of the sort!" Gail said firmly. "You panic and run, and that's that. I won't blame you. I'll even forgive you. There are people who just can't bear to be tied down, and I know you are one of them."

"Maybe until now," Larry agreed with her. "But right now I'm turning into the most confirmed carpetslippers, pipe, and fireside guy you ever saw. Oh, Gail, come on and marry me *now!*"

"Before you change your mind again?" Gail mocked him, her eyes merry, her cheeks flushed, and her heart beating so hard she felt sure that it must make a noise like bongo drums. "Oh, no, my lad. You're going to have plenty of time to sit down and think very hard before I do anything so permanent."

"Permanent?" He spoke the word as though he had never heard it before and wasn't quite sure what it meant. "You mean one of those lifetime sentences? Married until death do us part? You're that sort of girl?"

A little of the bright, sweet warmth that had possessed her when his arms had drawn her close and he had kissed her seeped away from her. He was looking terrified, she told herself, and a drop of bitterness was added to the joy she had known briefly.

"I'm afraid that's exactly the kind of girl I am, Larry," she said evenly. "And if the thought frightens you, you'd better stop and think fast. I don't want a marriage that's just a short-term lease. It's going to be forever and a day, or it's no good."

Larry studied her for a long moment, and then he stopped leaning on the chair. He straightened and moved away from her, his hands once more jammed into the pockets of his sports jacket. He was scowling thoughtfully as he walked away from her a pace or two and then turned and looked at her.

"Forever and a day, eh?" he mused as though he spoke his thoughts aloud. "I'm afraid I don't know very much about that kind of marriage, darling. Matter of fact, I don't believe I ever ran into one among my crowd. There, it's a 'Well, we'll have a go at it and if it doesn't work out—

well, there's always Paris in the spring or, if we're in a hurry, Mexico.' "

"I wouldn't want that kind of marriage, Larry, and you may as well know it now," she told him steadily. "With me, it would have to be for always, with all the old-fashioned things that probably seem very corny to you—like a home and children."

"I see," said Larry. "You're quite sure that's what you want?"

"Quite sure," Gail told him quietly; "as sure as I am that it isn't at all the kind of marriage you would want."

"Oh, now, wait a minute; give a fellow a chance to get his breath, will you?" protested Larry uneasily. "The whole idea is so new to me it takes a bit of getting used to. But you will have to give me credit for one thing, Gail, and that's being honest with you. I could tell you gaily, 'Oh, yes, forever and a day,' meanwhile keeping my fingers crossed behind my back, with the thought of all the quick-and-easy divorce mills all over the place. But I'm not going to do that. If you want it to be 'forever and a day,' then that's the way it's going to be."

Gail shook her head, her eyes meeting his steadily.

"Not until you are as sure of that as I am, Larry," she told him quietly. "For me, it just *has* to be that way. For you—well, you know better than I do what you want."

"Oh, I know what I want," Larry assured her instantly. "I want to marry you just as soon as it can be arranged."

"That's sweet of you, Larry, but we must wait until you are as sure as I am that it's to be—what did you call it?—a life sentence! What a nasty word to use for anything so beautiful as marriage to somebody you truly love."

Gail's brow was furrowed and her eyes were troubled. As Larry moved swiftly towards her, she once more put up her hands.

"No, Larry, no. Don't kiss me again. We've got to be sensible," she said, and stepped backward.

Larry's smile was warm and tender.

"All right, darling, you win," he said with a gentleness completely uncharacteristic of him. "I won't kiss you again. I won't touch you again until you are quite ready. But just remember that I love you and that you are the first girl I ever actually asked to marry me."

His eyes took her in from head to foot, and she felt as though they caressed her.

"We're going to have the most wonderful life together, darling," he told her huskily. "We're going places; we're going to see things; and I'm going to drape you with furs and beautiful clothes and hang jewels on you until you'll sparkle like a Christmas tree! Only I think I love you just the way you are!"

There were tears in her eyes and her smile was tremulous.

"Oh, Larry, if only you *really* meant that!" her voice was a small breath of sound scarcely strong enough to carry the weight of her emotion.

"I never in all my life meant anything so much," he said very low, his voice deep and vibrant with tenderness.

"I hope you really do, Larry," she told him huskily, and a light dawned swiftly in his eyes as he took a step toward her.

"Does that mean you will, darling?" he asked swiftly.

"I think so, Larry," she said foolishly. "We'll see. But for now let's wait a little while."

His mouth crooked in a rueful smile.

"Meaning you still aren't sure I really know my own mind, is that it?" he said, and waited for her answer.

"I'm not sure you think so, either," she confessed frankly. "And I have to be sure that *you* are sure."

"I can't blame you for that, darling." He was unexpectedly and uncharacteristically humble. "Well, take all the time you want—a week if you must, though I hope it won't be that long."

Gail laughed shakily, "A whole week? My goodness, you are patient, aren't you?"

"I'm anything else but," he told her swiftly. "It's only that I have been so rotten to you that I know it's going to take a while for you to learn to trust me again. But I give you my word of honor, Gail: I'll never let you down again. I want to marry you; and I hope you'll decide you want to marry me. For a little while or for life; that's for you to say."

"It will have to be for life, Larry, if I say it at all," she assured him firmly.

His smile was warm, tender, yet there was the faintest possible touch of mockery in it.

"The only girl I ever really wanted to marry, and she says it has to be a life sentence!" He laughed. "Well, so be it. I'd better run along now, I suppose. Come to think of it, I have a dinner date in Miami—but I'll break it if you like."

"Of course not," Gail protested, her eyes brimming with fond laughter. "Is she lovely and glamorous and sophisticated?"

Larry frowned thoughtfully.

"We-e-ell, yes, I suppose so; they usually are," he admitted frankly. "But she's not as sweet and good and adorable as you are. But then, nobody could be. You're something very special, Gail."

She stood for a long moment after he had gone. And then she put her hands over her face and gave herself up to her thoughts.

Chapter Eleven

Mary looked up at her as she came into the kitchen, and there was a curious look in Mary's dark brown eyes.

"Mr. Stillman staying for dinner?" she asked blandly.

"Oh, no, Mary, he's already gone," Gail answered. "He's taking Miss Donna's suitcase to her. And Mr. Troy won't be home for dinner, so I'll have mine in here with you, if I may."

"The table is already set in the dining room," Mary told her firmly. "You go on in; I'll bring your dinner."

"Yes, of course," said Gail, and wondered why it was that Mary's pronouncements always made her feel like a small, not very bright child. "Mr. Troy will be very late, Mary; I'll wait up for him and see he has his supper. I know you're tired, so you go on to bed."

She couldn't be sure, but she thought there was a faint twinkle in the inscrutable dark eyes.

"Yes, Miss Harrison," was all that Mary said. And before the look in her eyes, Gail blushed scarlet and went on into the dining room.

Mary served her as though the whole family had been there, and afterwards declined brusquely any offer of help clearing the table or doing the dishes.

Gail went on into the living room and curled up in a big chair with a new magazine.

She was sound asleep, curled uncomfortably in the big chair, when Troy came in some time after midnight. Haggard with weariness, grimy from his work with the machinery, Troy stood for a long, startled moment looking down at her. She looked so young, so defenseless, so vulnerable curled up there asleep. A deep tenderness was in his eyes as he looked at her, and then he bent and gently touched her shoulder.

"Hey, there, wake up!" His voice was touched with tender amusement. "Time little girls like you were tucked safely in their little beds!"

Gail started up, wide-eyed, confused for a moment. And then as she looked up at Troy, she stammered, "Oh, I must have fallen asleep."

"That's for sure, Troy teased her. "You were snoring up a storm!"

Gail gasped and color poured into her sleep-flushed face.

"Oh, I was not snoring. Golly, what a nasty thing to say," she protested hotly.

Troy laughed. "All right, I withdraw the remark. But you *were* sleeping very soundly," he answered. "What's the matter? Did Ellen turn you out of your room?"

"Oh, goodness, no. Ellen's not here," Gail told him. "She wanted to stay home, so Donna stayed with her. And Larry took Donna a suitcase with some things she needed. He said you'd be late, so I waited up for you because I thought you might be hungry."

"Well, thanks, Gail honey. That was very thoughtful of you. But I got a bite at a roadside diner. All I want now is about ten hours sleep," Troy told her, and barely managed to smother an enormous yawn.

"Oh, then you'd better go straight to bed, and I'll keep the children quiet in the morning so you can sleep as long as you like," Gail told him eagerly.

"Sounds wonderful but I have to be up at six in the morning," he told her ruefully. "We're beginning the burning of the cane fields, and all the independent owners work together, so it keeps us humping."

Gail stared at him in wide-eyed surprise.

"Burning the cane fields?" she repeated, puzzled. "But why, Troy?"

Troy laughed. "Well, it builds up the sugar content of the cane, burns out the leafy underbrush and makes it easier for the cutters," he answered. "Of course, about twenty-five to thirty thousand acres of the cane belong to the big sugar corporation. But we independent owners have a little over four thousand acres. Naturally, we allow the corporation to do the actual harvesting, the cutting and grinding. But we do the burning ourselves. Each plot of acreage is divided into forty acres that are burned at a time; all of us are on hand at each plot, because we can't afford to allow the fires to get beyond the cane fields. There are places in the Glades where the muck land itself will burn, and that's something to be avoided at all costs."

"I should think fire would destroy the sugar cane itself," Gail said. "But then I guess I just don't understand about an awful lot of things that people who live here take for granted."

Troy laughed again, his eyes warm and friendly. "Oh, well, you're a newcomer, Gail. It takes years and years ever to really begin to understand the things that go on here."

Gail said impulsively, "You love it here, don't you, Troy?"

"I can't imagine ever wanting to live anywhere else," he admitted frankly. "It's a strange, fascinating, sometimes cruel, sometimes gentle, but always wonderful place, with customs and people and ways all its own."

He broke off, gave her an abashed grin and warned, "It's much too late at night, and we both need sleep too much, for me to get started on a catalogue of all the Glades mean to me, Gail. The first free week or two I have, I'll try to tell you a little about it! Telling you the whole story would be a lifetime job."

"I do want to learn more about the Glades, Troy, because I think it's the most fascinating place I've ever seen!" she told him eagerly. "I can't think why people who have a lot of money to travel go rushing off to 'far-away places with strange-sounding names' when the Glades are within calling distance."

Troy laughed, "I must recommend you for membership in the Chamber of Commerce at Grove City," he teased her. "Time you were getting your beauty sleep, honey. Not that you need it, of course, but I need mine!"

"You work so hard, Troy," she mourned as she switched out the lights and they walked down the hall.

"It's not hard work, because I love it," he assured her quietly. "And nothing you love is hard work. Always remember that, Gail honey."

He paused at the door of the nursery, where she had stopped, and looked down at her.

"It was very sweet of you to wait up for me, honey," he said softly. "I'm grateful."

And then he bent his head and his lips brushed her cheek. The next moment he had gone on to his own room, while Gail stood at the nursery door staring after him, one hand creeping up to touch her cheek as though she expected to find there some tangible evidence of his kiss. . .

The following morning, Mary summoned her to the telephone, and Larry's voice spoke in her ear.

"Gail darling—" His voice was a caress that made her feel he had kissed her over the wire.

"Good morning, Larry."

She heard him laugh softly, and then his voice became brisk. "Look, darling, I have to be out of town for a few days, and I was afraid if I didn't call you and explain, you'd think things."

Gail admitted honestly, "I probably would have!"

"Well, don't!" he said sternly. "Those days are gone forever. And very soon I hope that when I go away, I won't go alone. You're going to make a marvelous travelling companion, darling. We're going to have a lifelong honeymoon!"

She was silent for a moment, and he asked anxiously, "We are, aren't we? You promised."

"I didn't promise anything, Larry, except to think about it," she stammered.

"Well, I'll be gone about a week. Less, if the business can be handled in less time than that.

And when I get back I expect you to have finished thinking and be ready to say, 'Why, yes, Larry, thanks a lot, I'd love to marry you!' " he said firmly. "Promise?"

"I promise to think very hard, Larry," she told him, and added impulsively, "And you must be thinking very hard, too."

"Oh, I've already finished thinking! I came to a very firm decision last night. This is *it*, darling, and it's for real, and it's for keeps!"

"And for life, Larry?"

"Well, yes, of course, since that's the way you said it had to be." He was laughing at her, she knew, and the thought gave her a warm, radiant happiness. "I'll have to run now, darling. See you all of a sudden."

The telephone clicked, and Gail put down the receiver with a hand that shook ever so slightly and went back to the patio where the children were playing.

She couldn't tell Troy or Donna anything about Larry's bewildering sudden proposal, she decided, until Larry came back and they could announce it together. And she caught her breath because she was taking it for granted, in her thoughts, that Larry's return would mean an announcement of their engagement.

She cringed at the thought of what Donna's and Troy's reaction might be. Would they think her a girl completely lacking in pride and self-respect after Larry's shameless treatment of her in the beginning? She didn't want Troy to think badly of her. But after all, Larry had begged for another chance, and she had given it to him, and what was so humiliating about that? Shouldn't she have forgiven him?

Oh, I'm so mixed up, she told herself, and was grateful for the sudden battle that sprang up between Cissy and Buddy, because it forced her to concentrate on arbitrating whatever childish dispute had brought it about. For the rest of the afternoon, she was busy with them so that there was no further time for private thoughts.

When Troy came home for dinner, Ellen and Donna were with him. Ellen looked gorgeously lovely in a thin, unrelieved black dress, her chestnut-colored hair a flame above the dense black, her face white and haggard. Donna was so gald to be back with the children that she insisted on giving them their bath and putting them to bed herself.

It developed that Troy had found a temporary manager for the camp, and that he and Donna had persuaded Ellen to stay at *La Casita* for at least a few days until she could decide what she wanted to do with the camp and with herself.

Troy was very gentle with her, and Ellen was a pallid, silent creature until after dinner, when suddenly she burst into wild, half-hysterical tears. She blamed herself because she hadn't been kinder to her father, because the last time they had been together they had quarreled furiously; and it was all that Troy and Donna could do to soothe her and get her to bed in the small, bright guest room that Mary had made ready for her.

She clung to Troy at the last, her tear-wet face pressed hard against his, her voice gusty with sobs as she said huskily, "Oh, Troy, my dearest, I don't know what I'd do without you! I hope I never have to learn how!"

Troy said very gently, his eyes tender, "You won't have to, darling. I'm going to take care of you from now on. You're to rest and relax and forget about everything. Just leave things to me."

"I will, Troy darling. Oh, I'm so glad that I can! I do love you so, Troy." Donna and Gail might as well not have been present as Ellen lifted her face and kissed him. Troy's arms tightened about her as he guided her down the hall to the room that was waiting for her.

Donna sat quite silent, her brows furrowed slightly, smoking, staring into space, and Gail could think of nothing to break the silence. When Troy came back, Donna looked up at him.

"Does she need me, do you think?" she asked quietly.

Troy shook his head, scowling as he crossed to a chair.

"She says she wants to be alone, poor kid," he answered.

Donna looked at the glowing tip of her cigarette, and after a moment she said thinly, as though the prospect did not please her too much, "So now you two can be married."

Troy looked up at her and then away.

"Well, yes, of course."

Donna nodded thoughtfully. "Bob has asked me to marry him. What do you think?"

Troy's smile was faint, but it erased the scowl.

"Would it matter what I think?" he asked mockingly.

Donna looked at him sharply, faintly resentful.

"Well, hasn't it always?" she demanded.

"I wasn't too crazy about your first marriage, remember?" Troy reminded her. "But it worked out all right."

"But you *do* like Bob, don't you?" Donna asked anxiously.

"Well, of course I do! He's one of the best! The question is not whether I like him, but whether you love him, isn't it?"

Neither of them seemed aware of Gail, who felt very uncomfortable but couldn't think of a way to leave the room without drawing too much attention to herself, and who could only sit where she was, an unwilling but helpless eavesdropper.

Donna looked across at Troy, and there was a softness in her smile, a dewiness in her eyes that lent emphasis to her quiet tone. "I love him very much."

"Then bless you both, Donna honey! A long life and a happy one," said Troy, and smiled warmly at her.

"Thanks, darling," said Donna radiantly. "With you and Ellen married, Bob and I will be living in town. And you, Gail, will come with us, of course. We'll love having you, and I can keep on working with Bob."

"That's very kind of you, Donna, but I have some plans of my own."

Donna frowned at her in surprise. "You have, Gail? What are they?"

Gail swung a glance at Troy, who was watching her with a curious, inscrutable look. Color poured into her face as she looked back and met Donna's eyes.

"Larry has asked me to marry him," Gail stammered.

"What?" Donna gasped. "Again?"

Troy was watching Gail, saying nothing, but his hands had clenched into tight fists, and his jaw was set and hard.

"Well, he said he realized now he really did love me." Gail's voice stumbled and fell into the pool of silence between them.

"And then he immediately took off for New York, or some far place," snapped Donna, and there was irritation touched with disgust in her eyes. "Oh, Gail honey, for heaven's sake, haven't you learned yet that you can't trust that slimy beast? How many times are you going to let him make a fool of you? You know darned well the only reason he came back was because he was curious to know what Troy and I saw in you. The fact that you gave him a brush-off aroused his competitive instinct, and he immediately set about trying to coax you to trust him again. Gail, you can't be such a simple-minded little fool as to believe anything he says."

"That's enough, Donna," said Troy sharply. "Gail is neither simple-minded nor a fool. And if she's convinced that she can trust Larry, that's her business."

"And what a business!" snapped Donna hotly. "I'm very disappointed in you, Gail. I thought you had more pride, more self-respect—"

"I said that's enough, Donna!" Troy cut in sharply. "Let her alone. If she wants Larry—"

"That's not the question," snapped Donna. "The question is, does Larry want her? And we both know the answer is a big fat no!"

Gail was scarlet with embarrassment, and confusion and tears were threatening her as she forced her voice to some semblance of steadiness.

"He said he did," she insisted miserably.

"Oh, sure he would! He can't bear to think there's any girl anywhere who's not ready to fall into his arms the minute he opens them. And then he gets a grand laugh out of running like a scared rabbit while she falls flat on her face!" Donna raged. "Honestly, Gail, I'd think you'd have had enough of him."

"Donna, I've told you to stop it, and I mean it!" Troy caught Donna by the shoulder and shook her. "Now let her alone. Go ahead and marry your Bob, and get someone else to look after the children."

"You don't think I'm trying to keep her from making a fool of herself just so I'll have someone I can trust to look after the babes, Troy? You couldn't be such a fool! I want to see Gail married and living happily ever after, but you and I both know there isn't a chance of that with Larry."

"I think," said Troy firmly, and turned her about, his hands on her shoulders, "that it's time you trotted off to bed. In the morning I'll expect you to apologize to Gail and wish her every happiness. Now, scoot!"

As if she'd been no older than Cissy, he guided her to the door and down the hall to her own room. As he came back toward the living room, he met Gail creeping miserably toward her own room.

"Gail honey," he said very gently, taking her hand and leading her back to the living room, "I'm truly sorry Donna blew up! She didn't mean it."

"She did, Troy, and I suppose you, too, think I'm lacking in pride and—and self-respect." Gail was fighting hard against the tears that were threatening to overwhelm her. And as though she had been Cissy, or a younger sister, Troy's arms gathered her comfortingly close.

"I don't think anything of the kind, Gail honey, and you know it," Troy soothed her. "I have known Larry for a long, long time. I know what a charmer he can be when he wants to be. And I know, too, that one of these days he'll get his come-uppance and find a girl he can't leave. And I think maybe he's found her in you, Gail."

She could only lift her eyes swimming in tears and attempt vainly to thank him.

Troy seemed suddenly to realize that she was in his arms. He let her go, and stood for a moment, his hands jammed deeply into his pockets, scowling thoughtfully down at her.

"Did you know that he left for New York on the noon plane?" he asked after a moment.

"Oh, yes," Gail answered. "He called me to say goodbye and tell me that he'd be gone a week—"

Troy grinned ruefully.

"I'm glad to hear that!" he said frankly. "I was afraid that he'd just taken fright and started running again."

"I would have thought that if he hadn't called me," she admitted huskily. "I told him that we must be very sure and that it would take some thinking before I said I'd marry him. So if he'd just gone off without calling me, I'd have thought what you and Donna thought."

There was a brief silence between them, and then she looked up at him and said unsteadily, "I can't tell you how glad I am that you don't despise me."

Troy scowled at the word.

"Despise you, Gail? Why, how could I?"

"Well, Donna does. She thinks I haven't any pride."

"Donna was very tired, and she will tell you in the morning that she is sorry for her bad manners, and that she hopes you and Larry will be very happy," Troy assured her firmly. "Now you run along to bed, and tomorrow we'll all feel much better about everything."

He smiled down at her, and for a breathless moment the memory of last night when his lips had brushed her cheek so lightly was so vivid that she waited for that touch again. Then color poured into her face and she went swiftly out of the living room and to her own room, where she dropped down on the edge of the bed, her face hidden behind her shaking hands.

She was still sitting on the edge of her bed when there was a gentle tap at the door and Donna's voice asked softly, "Gail, honey, are you asleep?"

"Oh, no, Donna, come in." Gail steadied her voice and stood up, hoping that Donna had not come to continue her denunciation of Larry and of Gail for her faith in him.

Donna came in, wrapped in a navy blue robe, looking penitent and smiling warmly.

"Gail, honey, I couldn't go to sleep before I told you how sorry I am that I was such a witch," she said eagerly. "I know I had no right to say anything."

"Oh, please, Donna!" Gail was radiant with relief that there was to be no more unpleasantness. "I know you meant it as good advice."

Donna's face was touched with a rueful smile.

"And I don't know anything more unpleasant than to offer unsolicited advice, good, bad or indifferent," she said frankly, and came to perch on the side of the bed and put her arm around Gail. "It's only, honey, that I'm so very fond of you, I didn't want to see you let yourself in for more of the treatment Larry gave you in the beginning."

She drew Gail down beside her and went on, "You see, Gail, I've known for a long time that I was going to marry Bob as soon as he got around to asking me. And, of course, Troy and Ellen have been engaged for ages. Now that Ellen is free and they can be married, he'll bring her here to live, and the babes and I will move into Bob's house. It's a big house and there's plenty of room. All along, I planned that you should go with us. So I didn't want you to feel that you *had* to marry Larry for shelter! That you'll always have with Bob and me, and we'll love having you."

Deeply touched, humbly grateful, Gail stammered, "That's very kind."

"Phooey! Kind my foot," Donna dismissed the thought airily. "Don't get it into your head that I'm offering you charity or being kind to you, you silly child! I shall need you even more than I've needed you here! You'll be doing me a tremendous favor, because I want to keep on working with Bob. And knowing how devoted you are to the babes, and how much they love you—well, I can work with a free and untroubled mind. So unless you really *are* in love with Larry—" She broke off and studied Gail for a long moment before she asked quietly, "*Are* you, Gail?"

Gail said honestly, "I don't know for sure, Donna. I guess I don't know much about being in love."

"About as much, I'd say, as Cissy does." Donna smiled at her. "Well, don't be in any rush about deciding, honey. For when you are in love, you know it. Bells ring, birds swing, and you float on air if you so much as hear his name; and when he touches you—" Her smile finished for her "Just think about it honey. Think real hard about it before you decide."

"Oh, I promised him I would," Gail answered earnestly. "And he's going to think hard about it, too."

"I bet he is," Donna murmured so softly that Gail could pretend she had not heard. And then

Donna stood up. "Well, I've got to get some sleep, and so must you. I just wanted you to know that you don't have to rush out and marry the first man who asks you just to be sure you'll have a roof over your head."

She brushed Gail's cheek with her lips, gave her shoulder a little squeeze, said good night and departed.

Chapter Twelve

A week passed swiftly. There was no word from Larry, and Troy and Donna appeared elaborately unaware of the fact, though as each day slid by, Gail felt an increasing uneasiness.

Ellen stayed on at *La Casita,* because Bob was disposing of the camp for her, and at a very handsome price. Troy was working hard, leaving before the others were up, often not coming home to dinner at all. There were evenings when Gail would awaken from sleep near midnight or afterwards and hear the sound of his car in the drive, his quiet footsteps in the house.

One afternoon near the end of the week, when Gail was on the patio with the children, Ellen came strolling out. Clad in the briefest of white shorts and a halter, her sun-tanned body looked sleek and smooth and very lovely. Her hair was burnished chestnut in the sunshine, and as she dropped into a long wicker garden chair, she drew her sun-tanned legs up under her and lit a cigarette.

Gail waited for her to speak.

Ellen was regarding the jungle that pressed close beyond the patio wall, and suddenly she burst out explosively, "How I hate this place!"

Wide-eyed, Gail asked, "You mean *La Casita?*"

"I mean the Glades!" said Ellen harshly. "Every blooming, blasted square inch of it; all the swamps, the bogs, the wild beasts, every single thing about it. I can't wait to get my hands on the check for Ibis and get away. And I hope devoutly never to set eyes on any part of it again."

Gail stared at her, shocked.

"But, Ellen, you and Troy are going to be married."

Ellen's sombre eyes slued around to Gail's face.

"So?" she mocked.

"So this is Troy's home and he loves it. How can you live somewhere else if he is here?"

"So Troy's going to sell out, too, and we'll live somewhere else," Ellen said with such assurance that Gail could not find words to answer her. "I want a place where there are paved streets, highways, people, shops, civilization! New York, I think, or perhaps California. I haven't quite decided yet."

"Does Troy know how you feel?" asked Gail at last.

Ellen smiled, a malicious unmirthful smile.

"Of course not," she mocked. "You think I'm a fool? Time enough to tell him after we're married. Because we are going to be married, Gail. Make no mistake about that."

"I wasn't going to," Gail answered, so bewildered by the unexpectedness of the conversation that she could only sit and stare at Ellen.

"Troy's worked his heart out here, and he's got the property built up to the point where he can get a very handsome price for it," Ellen went on. "The way things are now, he keeps plowing the profits back into more land, more cattle, more sugar cane; more of everything except a decent living in a place where there are the comforts, even luxuries that all women want. I am so sick of the kind of men who come to places like Ibis; the women in their too tight slacks, and their attitude that they are 'roughing it' when they leave off their nail polish! I want beautiful clothes, a fine car, an apartment in a good neighborhood. I want to go out to dinner at an expensive restaurant, done up in furs and jewels and a gown that makes all the other women hate me."

Gail was still for a long moment, and then she said uneasily, "But, Ellen, Troy loves it here."

Ellen glanced at her and then away, and there was an ugly twist to her lovely mouth.

"Troy loves *me*," she said. "And because he loves me, he wants me to be happy. I've got it all planned. We'll spend our honeymoon in New York, and while we're there, I'll persuade him to get in touch with Bob and have Bob sell all his Glades properties. And *then*—" she threw out her arms in an expansive gesture and lifted her face toward the sun and closed her eyes—"we'll begin really living."

"But, Ellen," protested Gail, wide-eyed, "this is Troy's home. Why, he came here when he was just a small boy, with his father. They worked very hard, and when his father died, Troy felt it was almost a sacred trust for him to carry out all his father's plans and develop some of his own. Why, what would Troy do in New York?"

Ellen studied her curiously, her eyes narrowed slightly.

"I really can't see that's any of your affair," she mocked, and there was no effort to mask the malice in her eyes and in her tone. "Troy's intelligent; he'll find something to do. And he'll do it because he wants me to be happy."

"But, Ellen, don't *you* want *him* to be happy?" asked Gail spiritedly.

The malice in Ellen's eyes deepened.

"That, too, is no concern of yours," she answered swiftly. "Oh, he'll be happy. I'll see to that!"

"Away from the Glades—" Gail began.

"Away from the Glades, and the miserable existence I've always known here, we'll both be happy," Ellen snapped, and added, "I suppose you'll run straight to Troy and tell him what I'm planning?"

Gail stiffened and there were sparks in her eyes.

"Why should I?" she demanded.

Ellen's mouth curled in a smile that robbed it of all its beauty.

"Oh, because you are in love with him and you'd like to have him for yourself, of course." She threw the words at Gail as though they had been small, sharp stones meant to cut and bruise.

Gail caught her breath and her eyes went wide with shock.

"*I'm* in love with Troy?" she gasped incredulously.

"Well, of course, you silly goose!" snapped Ellen. "Didn't you know that? I have, from the first day you came to Ibis. But it didn't worry me, because I've got first claim on Troy. And he wouldn't waste a second glance on you, anyway. So trot along and tell him all I've said, if you like, and I'll tell him you are lying, and why."

Gail was too dazed, too bewildered by the warmth that was enveloping her like a rich velvet cloak to manage an answer.

Ellen studied her for a long moment.

"So you threw him the information that Larry Stillman wanted to marry you, just in the hope that it would jolt Troy into realizing he was in love with you, too," she accused Gail bitterly. "But it didn't work out that way, did it? Troy is loyal and faithful; he has always been in love with me."

"The first time we met, you told me he was not in love with you, remember?" Gail pointed out.

Ellen shrugged carelessly.

"Oh, that was before I was free," she mocked. "He knew I couldn't marry him as long as I had my father to look after. But now we are both free. And we are going to have a wonderful time! With the money I'll get for Ibis, and the money Bob can get him for his properties, we can travel, see the world, have a grand and glorious time. And after what I've been through, drudging and working and doing without all the things I am entitled to—" Once more she flung her arms wide as though the prospect were one that she scarcely dared try to visualize.

Gail could only sit, stricken, watching her.

Ellen yawned at last, got up and strolled into the house without another word. And Gail could only sit and turn over in her mind the amazing things Ellen had said. The most amazing of all had been the accusation that she, Gail, was in love with Troy!

And more amazing still was her realization that it was true.

Cissy stumbled against her knee, looking up at her with wide eyes and demanding attention. Gail put her own thoughts away in a safe, secure corner of her heart, reminding herself that she was there to look after the children; not break her heart over a man who was engaged to another girl, and whom she had been fool enough to learn to love!

When Donna came home that evening, Bob came with her and handed over, with laughing ceremony, the cashier's check for the sale of Ibis.

"That's the down payment, Ellen," he told her. "They wanted to pay the rest at the rate of three thousand a year, payable semi-annually, for five years. I thought you would like having an assured income in addition to the down payment."

Ellen studied the check, her eyes wide and dark.

"Twenty thousand dollars!" she breathed aloud, awed. "It's all the money in the world!"

Bob smiled at her, and Donna's eyes were moist.

"Well, not quite, Ellen," said Bob. "Remember, twice a year there will be fifteen hundred more for the next five years! I'll see that it's paid promptly and deliver it to you with due ceremony."

It was one of the few evenings recently that Troy had been home for dinner, and he beamed happily at Ellen, enjoying her delight.

"This calls for a celebration! It should be champagne, of course, but I'm afraid the wine cellar at

La Casita doesn't quite run to champagne. But there's wine, I'm sure."

Ellen, dreamily studying the check, said eagerly, "Oh, we can have champagne when we get to New York, Troy."

Troy stared at her, puzzled.

"Who's going to New York, honey?" he asked.

Ellen looked up at him brightly, and Gail realized that Ellen had spoken without thinking. But she laughed and covered her carelessness with a gay, "Oh, aren't we going to New York on our honeymoon? You promised, remember?"

"Then we can't be married until spring, darling," Troy told her firmly, "unless you want to have a delayed honeymoon. I can't possibly get away, even for a week-end, until spring."

Ellen lowered her eyes to the check and shrugged.

"Then we'll be married in the spring," she agreed. "I really *should* run up to New York and do some shopping."

"Oh, no, you don't," Troy protested, and dropped an arm about her shoulder and drew her close. "You can go trousseau-shopping in Miami Beach. You're not going to New York without me!"

Ellen laughed up at him.

"Of course not, darling." Ellen's voice was practically a coo. "New York wouldn't be any fun without you!"

Troy kissed her lightly, and Ellen drew away from him and looked at the check again.

"I *do* need a new car and a few rags, so I'll go over to Miami Beach tomorrow and do a spot of shopping," she said gaily.

"Watch yourself in Miami Beach, Ellen." Bob laughed. "That check will shrink like snow in July if you aren't careful!"

Ellen laughed. "Oh, well there's more where this came from," she answered. "And when Troy and I are married, I'll be *his* financial responsibility, so I can look at this as just pin money!"

Troy chuckled and looked down at the check. "Unless you'd like to give me a wedding present," he suggested gaily.

"Such as what, for instance?" asked Ellen suspiciously.

"Well, there's a herd of Brahma calves going at a very good price, because the cattleman is overstocked—" began Troy, a twinkle dancing in his eyes.

Ellen wrenched herself away from him, her eyes blazing.

"Not one cent of this is going to buy one more blasted animal for this place or another inch of land," she burst out so sharply that they all stared at her in shocked surprise.

"Well, look, I'm sorry," Troy said, nettled by Ellen's reaction. "It was only a joke, honey, and a very feeble one. I have already bought the calves, and they are to be paid for when the sugar harvest is in. I got the money from the bank."

Ellen stared at him, her eyes angry.

"You've bought more cattle, Troy? You've got more now than you have pasturage for," she snapped.

Troy's eyes on her now were quite cool, and there was no longer the vestige of a twinkle in them.

"So I've leased some land from Mary's tribe to pasture the new calves," he stated flatly.

Ellen flung out a hand, a frown of annoyance between her brows.

"But, Troy darling," she protested, "you work so hard, and you never allow yourself a moment's pleasure—"

"Because I get pleasure from the work."

"Oh, I suppose so," Ellen yielded ungraciously. "But you're going to be an old man before your time. It just isn't fair! You make a profit on the citrus and then you plow it into more land, more cattle. Why?"

Troy was studying her curiously as though seeing her for the first time.

"Building for the future; what else?" he asked grimly.

There was the sudden sharp clamor of the telephone, and Donna, beside Gail, murmured barely above her breath, "Saved by the bell!" as she rose to answer the summons.

A moment later she was back to say, "It's for you, Gail. Larry is calling."

Gail stared at her for a moment before she got to her feet, and Ellen gave a brittle, contemptuous laugh.

"So he's come back, has he?" she mocked.

"He's calling from New York," Donna answered her curtly as Gail hurried out of the room.

Larry's voice was warm and eager as he spoke in her ear.

"Hi, sweetie," he greeted her. "Did you miss me?"

"Yes, but of course I wasn't surprised that you went away."

"Now, you've got a mean, suspicious mind," Larry scolded her tenderly. "Look, Precious, I was on a skiing house party in Vermont, and we got snowed in. Telephone lines down, no communication with the outside world for five days! Fortunately, we had plenty of food and fuel, so we didn't really suffer, except that I was worried about you."

"You needn't have been."

"I was worried about what you might think when I didn't remind you that I was waiting for you to make up your mind about me," he cut in swiftly. "Look, Baby, I can't get a seat on a plane for a day or two, but I'll be there the minute I can make it. Love me?"

"I'm not quite sure," Gail admitted with painful honesty.

"Well, you'd better be, because I'm sure! I've had time to do that thinking you warned me about, and you know how it comes out? It comes out that I want to marry you more than I've ever wanted anything! I'll see you in a day or two, and I'm bringing you a lot of pretties! What would you like most?"

"Whatever you want to bring."

She heard Larry give a mocking groan. "You missed your cue, sweetie. You were supposed to say, 'The thing I want most is you!'"

Gail managed a small laugh, sharply conscious of the others in the living room, keeping quiet so that she could take the long distance phone call.

"I'm sorry," she said lightly. "Just consider that I didn't miss my cue and said what you expected—"

"You can't possibly say, 'I love you, darling, and I'm counting the hours until I see you again'?" he suggested hopefully.

"I'm afraid I can't, right now," she admitted huskily.

"Oh, there's somebody else there?" demanded Larry jealously.

"Well, of course, Larry. Why wouldn't there be?"

"Oh, the family, eh? And they aren't any too crazy about me, anyway. Oh, well, I'll whisk you away from there before the end of next week, so that doesn't matter," said Larry firmly. "Look, I have to run now. I'll see you all of a sudden, Precious, as soon as I can get a plane seat."

She put down the receiver and stood for a moment before she drew a long breath, braced herself and walked back to the living room where the others were waiting.

"What was his alibi?" asked Ellen silkily.

Troy shot her a swift, hard glance, but Gail answered quietly, "A skiing party that got snowbound in Vermont. He'll be here as soon as he can get a plane reservation."

Ellen laughed, that soft, silky laugh that was the very essence of insolent doubt.

"You want to bet?" she drawled softly. And once again Troy's eyes on her were cold, startled, as though he had never before suspected her of such malice.

"If we want any dinner, we'd better let Mary know," said Donna briskly, and smiled warmly at Bob as he offered her his arm and they led the way out of the living room to the dining room.

Ellen claimed Troy's arm, slipping both her hands through it and drawing herself close, smiling up at him intimately. Troy gave her a cool glance and offered his other arm to Gail, who accepted it hesitantly, feeling the inimical regard of Ellen's eyes as they followed Donna and Bob.

When they were all settled at the table, and

Mary had served the fruit cup, Ellen propped her check up against a water goblet and looked defiantly about the group that was watching her.

"I know you all think I'm perfect zany to be so excited by this check," she accused them.

Donna said lightly, "Don't look at me! If I had a check for twenty grand in my hot, grubby little paws, I'd frame it and make a household god out of it."

"Well, I'm not going to frame it," said Ellen. "I'm going to cash it and spend it riotously! After all, I never had more than twenty dollars for myself at one time in my whole life. And even then I had to fight my conscience before spending it for myself. There were always so many things that were needed desperately at Ibis. But now—" She drew a deep, joyous breath, and one finger touched the check caressingly.

She looked once more about the group and beamed.

"Tomorrow I'm going to have the biggest thrill of my whole life," she announced radiantly. "I'm going to buy a new car, and then I'm going to drive old Betsy into the nearest canal and watch happily as she sinks from view."

Bob said lightly, "That's against the law, Ellen. The authorities are very fussy about such things. Why don't you trade Betsy in on your new car?"

"The salesman would sneer in my face, and

then I'd probably smack him and wind up in jail." Ellen laughed and leaned toward Troy. "You'll help me choose my new car, won't you, darling? We'll leave early and have the whole day."

"Sorry," said Troy briefly. "I won't be able to take a day off. I'm sure you'll make a wise choice, though."

Ellen glared at him furiously. "But, Troy darling, I'll get cheated if I go alone!" she wailed.

Bob said pleasantly, "If I could be of assistance, and if you'd trust my judgment, I'd be happy to drive you over."

"Hi, now, wait a minute," protested Donna jealously. "You can't take a whole day off, either. I won't permit it "

Bob laughed and reached a hand to cover hers where it lay on the table beside her plate.

"Angel-face, you're going, too, of course," he told her firmly. "I have to see Old Man Forbes tomorrow, and I'll want you to take notes and see the old tycoon doesn't wiggle out of that agreement with Mason that we insisted he make."

"Oh," said Donna, completely mollified, "as long as I'm to go, too, then you can have the day off."

"That's very kind of you, ma'am!" said Bob with mock humility, his eyes on her very warm and tender.

"Incidentally, I have some shopping to do, and it will all work out beautifully." Donna's smile was equally warm and tender, and Gail saw her hand turn beneath Bob's until their fingers were clasped.

Chapter Thirteen

There was a holiday air about Donna and Ellen the next morning while they awaited Bob's arrival. Troy was gone long before they breakfasted. Gail had heard his car leaving the drive a little before six. Later, when she had bathed and fed the children and had them out on the patio for their morning sun bath and play, she sat for a long moment looking about her at the fresh, sun-swept glory of the morning.

The air was soft and warm, fragrant with the scent of orange blossoms from the grove just beyond the edge of the jungle. There was, underlying the scent of the blossoms, a faint, tangy fragrance that she had learned was the scent of the jungle itself. Geraniums surrounding the sun dial added their own smell; birds darted and swung like bits of bright-hued jewels. Behind her was the house, long and low, its cream-colored walls splashed with the brilliant beauty of bougainvillea.

Oh, it was so beautiful! Surely, she told herself, it was the most beautiful, the most fascinating place in all the world. How could Ellen possibly want to trade it for a big city like New York? And how would Troy adjust there? Somehow she couldn't believe that he ever would.

Bob's arrival startled her out of her thoughts, and Donna and Ellen came quickly out of the house, dressed for Miami in smartly cut sports frocks, even wearing hats: microscopic bits of fluff that did little except enhance the beauty of their hair.

Donna said to Gail, "I do wish you could come with us, honey. It looks as if it might be fun."

Gail smiled at her. "I'd rather stay here, thanks a lot. I'll never get tired of all this. It's so beautiful."

Ellen's mouth curled in a faint sneer, but she said nothing as she went on and got into the car.

Donna swooped on the children, hugging them tightly, and putting them down again as she said brightly, "You be good babes now, and don't give Gail any trouble, and Mommie'll bring you a present."

Gail watched as they all got into the car, and threw up her hand to return their waves of leavetaking. When the car had vanished and the sound of it had died away on the bright morning, she went back to her chair and to her thoughts.

They were confused this morning, she admitted. But then, she had to add quite honestly, they had been ever since the night when Larry had held her close and had offered that proposal of marriage. She hadn't been willing to take him seriously then; she was none too sure that she should now. Yet his phone call from New York last night had surely sounded as though he were very serious indeed.

The day passed quietly, as it always did when Gail and the children and Mary were alone at *La Casita*. It was dusk when Troy came back; he smiled at Gail and the children as he paused a moment.

"I suppose the others aren't back yet," he said lightly. "They'll probably stay in town for dinner."

Before he finished, Bob's car slid into the drive, and Bob and Donna got out and came through the patio gate, laden with parcels.

"Where's Ellen?" asked Troy, puzzled.

"She checked into a hotel on the beach," said Donna briskly, and did not quite meet his eyes. "She was much too excited to be willing to come back with us and very annoyed that Bob and I wouldn't stay in town and take her for a round a night-clubbing."

"I suppose she bought the car?" asked Troy, as though only mildly interested.

"Oh, bru-ther!" Donna raised one hand in a little gesture of despair. "It's a good thing Bob was along; he and I together barely managed to talk her out of a Rolls-Royce! She finally settled for a Cadillac convertible *and* a white mink stole. I hate to think what the two purchases did to her precious twenty grand. And when I left her, she was surrounded by eager saleswomen in the Beach's most exclusive *and* expensive shop. Chances are we'll have to go over and lend her money to buy gas to get back to *La Casita*."

Troy grinned. "Oh, well, she's had a rough time all her life. About time she was beginning to have a little fun."

"Well, that's something you don't have to worry about, Brother Mine! That one is going to have fun—not little, but large fat gobs of it! Bob introduced her to a very personable gent, who's delighted to squire her around to all the fabulous places she wants to see tonight. And he's sufficiently well-heeled to be able to pick up the tab even for a gal who has suddenly developed the most expensive tastes."

Bob said apologetically, "He's really quite a decent sort, Troy."

Troy laughed. "I'm sure he is, Bob, or you wouldn't have introduced him to her; I hope she'll have a happy evening. And now I'll have to go and change before dinner. You're staying for dinner, Bob. Mary would be insulted if you didn't!"

"Well, we wouldn't want that to happen, would we? Thanks, I'd like to very much," Bob answered, laughing as Donna went to the children and began displaying the presents she had brought them.

"I knew they should have been in bed by now, Donna," Gail said apologetically. "But they begged to stay up until you came home."

"Well, I should hope so," said Donna gaily. She lifted Cissy and set her in Bob's arms, who reached for her eagerly. "Will you bring the packages, Gail? Bob will help me get them to bed, won't you, darling?"

"There's nothing I'd like better, until it becomes a nightly affair," said Bob. And, cradling the pleased Cissy, he turned and walked toward the house.

Donna, scooping Buddy up in her arms, holding him very close, smiled at Gail through a mist of happy tears.

"Oh, Gail honey, isn't it wonderful that the babes are going to have a father? We've been alone so long," she whispered. And then, made uncomfortable by the tears, she turned, carrying the little boy close, and followed Bob and Cissy into the house.

Gail sat on for a little and then, with a small shrug that tried hard to dismiss the growing uneasiness in her heart, rose, collected the packages and moved toward the house with them.

She had showered, changed from her daytime garb of a gingham play-suit into her pink linen sheath, and was coming into the living room, where only Troy waited, when he turned and stared at her, studying her with a look that brought a swift, startled throbbing to her heart.

"You look very pretty, Gail," he said quietly. "But then you always do. Matter of fact, I don't think I'd realized quite how pretty you are until just lately."

Gail could only stare at him, and he turned sharply away as though to avoid her eyes. Over his shoulder, in an entirely different voice, he asked, "Bob and Donna are getting the children ready for bed, aren't they?"

"Yes. She wanted to give them their supper and get them to bed herself, and Bob seemed glad to help," Gail answered and blushed at the utter inanity of the words.

"I suppose Bob feels he ought to get in training," he said after a moment. "But since you are going to be living with them—"

"But I'm not, Troy," she protested. "Didn't you know?"

"Larry?" he asked, still without looking at her.

"I'm not sure, Troy. But I won't be with Bob and Donna, I'm sure of that."

"Donna will be disappointed."

"I don't think so. I think she'll want to give up working in the office with Bob and be a homemaker and a mother. Bob's been alone for a long time; his house is closed up. I imagine it will be a full-time job for Donna to make it a home for him again."

Troy nodded, his brows furrowed slightly.

"And of course as to you and Larry—I want the greatest possible happiness for you, Gail honey! I've never known a girl I thought deserved it more," he said slowly, deeply in earnest. "If Larry can give you that happiness, then here's to both of you."

He smiled, lifted his glass and saluted her with a smile.

Gail felt color warm her face, and her eyes could not quite meet his.

"That's kind of you, Troy. Thank you," she said.

There was the sound of laughter from the hall, and Donna and Bob came in, his arm about her, his face bent toward hers that was lifted to his. As they entered the living room he glanced at Troy and Gail.

"I'm not only getting the loveliest wife in the world; I'm getting two of the most beautiful children." He beamed. "How lucky can a guy get?"

Donna winked merrily at Gail.

"Let's not tell him, Gail, that they can also be

the most exasperating small fry any father had to cope with."

"Let's not," Gail agreed, smiling, "because they really are adorable, and I'm sure he'll be able to handle them."

"Well," said Donna, accepting the Martini that Bob handed her and lifting it in a toast, "here's to all of us. May we never be less happy than we are at this moment."

"I'll drink to that," said Bob firmly.

When Mary came to announce dinner, Donna turned to her eagerly.

"Oh, Mary, Miss Ellen wants Johnny to have her old car," she announced.

Mary stiffened and her copper-skinned face was blank.

"Why would she want that?" she demanded suspiciously.

"Oh, I suppose she likes Johnny," Donna answered.

"She hates him." Mary's voice drowned Donna's. "Miss Ellen likes nobody but Miss Ellen."

Before Donna could answer, Mary turned her dark eyes on Bob.

"Will they let Johnny keep his job?" she demanded.

"You mean the new owners of Ibis?" asked Bob. "Well, of course they will. Johnny's the best guide at the camp."

"Johnny's the best guide in the Glades," Mary

corrected him firmly, "when white people leave him alone and don't try to get him in trouble."

"Johnny's a master mechanic, Mary," said Troy. "He'll have that car running like a Glades bobcat."

Mary nodded. "Sure he will, and he needs the car. I'll let him know he can come and get it. Did Miss Ellen give you papers saying it's his car, Mr. Jordan?"

Bob drew an envelope from his pocket and held it out to her.

"Everything he'll need to prove ownership is there, Mary," he said.

Mary took the envelope, smoothed it caressingly, and nodded.

"Please thank Miss Ellen for both of us," she said, and turned away.

"Well, that's not exactly what you'd call the most grateful acceptance of a gift," Donna said ruefully.

"I suppose Mary feels Johnny's earned it, and I think she's right," Troy answered. "After all, Johnny and the others who work with him are chiefly responsible for the camp's success. People know that if they come to Ibis they're sure to have good hunting or good fishing; Johnny's guides guarantee that."

"I suppose," Donna agreed, and slipped her hand through Bob's arm. "Shall we eat? I'm starving."

Two evenings later, they had just finished dinner and were moving into the living room. Bob was there again, and he and Donna had been making plans for their approaching wedding, when there was the sound of a car in the drive. It was driven too rapidly, brought to a too sudden halt as the spraying of shell on the drive told them. There came the sound of gay laughter and quick footsteps, and then through the open door Ellen and Larry came swiftly.

Arrogantly aware of her beauty, Ellen paused in the doorway: an exquisite vision in ice-blue brocade that wrapped her body as though it had been painted on her; a white mink stole which slipped negligently from her bare shoulders; her hair done in an intricate coiffure that only an expensive beautician could have managed. There was the gleam of sapphires and diamonds at her throat and at her ears. She looked smooth, sleek, sophisticatedly beautiful, a far cry indeed from the Ellen Matthews who had so short a time before conducted the affairs of the Ibis Fishing and Hunting Camp.

Larry stood a pace behind her, looking down at her with an indulgent grin, his eyes laughing.

"O.K., Beautiful," he drawled. "They've been devastated by the sight of you. You've made your entrance. Now move aside and let me find my girl, will you?"

Ellen laughed up at him as he brushed past her,

caught Gail in his arms and held her close for a moment, his mouth on hers. Gail was painfully aware of the eyes of the others upon them as she struggled to free herself.

"Oh, please, Larry!" she pleaded in an agony of confusion, when she could free her mouth from the pressure of his own.

Larry, his arms still holding her, laughed at her confusion.

"Don't be shy, Precious," he teased her fondly. "We're among friends. They all know we're going to be married as soon as it can be arranged."

"Of course," said Donna smoothly, taking pity on Gail's scarlet-faced embarrassment. "Matter of fact, Bob and I were just discussing our own wedding plans. Care to make it a double wedding, Ellen?"

Ellen had dropped the white mink stole, had perched herself on the arm of the sofa and was lighting a cigarette in a long carved ivory holder.

"Thanks, Donna, but no, thanks," she drawled sweetly.

Donna shrugged carelessly.

"Oh, well, since you and Troy aren't going to be married until spring—" she began.

"Since Troy and I aren't going to married, period." Ellen delivered the bombshell with an almost casual air. Then she looked from one startled face to another, her eyes resting longest on Troy's face, that was a controlled mask. "Aren't you pleased, Troy, that I'm letting you off the hook?"

"I'm afraid I hadn't quite considered that I was on your hook," Troy told her, spacing his words deliberately, his expression and his tone polite, colorless.

Ellen studied him, a small, not too pleasant smile curling her beautifully colored mouth, her eyes narrowed.

"You're not in love with me, Troy, so don't pretend to be broken-hearted," she drawled. "And I know now that I'm not in love with you, that I never have been! Oh, I thought I was. As long as I was penniless and tied down to Ibis, you looked like the man of my dreams. But somehow I know you'd never be willing to sell this place and go to New York to live."

Troy barked in savage anger, "Well, you were perfectly right. I have no such intention."

Ellen nodded slowly. "I thought at first I could wear you down until you were willing," she admitted frankly. "But now that I've had a taste of fun and good times and civilization, I know that you wouldn't be much fun even if I *could* wear you down. I'm seeing clearly now, and therefore I'm turning you loose so Gail can have you."

Larry, who had been listening to her, amused rather than shocked, started as though he'd been struck.

201

"Hi, now, wait a minute," he protested sharply. "Gail's going to marry me!"

Ellen's eyes were fastened on Gail's face, and she smiled a slow, twisted smile.

"Is she?" she drawled. "Ask her, Larry."

"I've already asked her and she said she would," Larry protested.

"You'd better ask her again, to be sure." Ellen's voice dripped with sarcasm. "That was when she thought Troy was in love with me; before she realized that Troy loved her, not me."

Gail protested wildly, "That's not true!" She looked up into Troy's face, caught her breath at what she saw in his eyes and asked faintly, "*Is* it?"

Troy reached for her, drew her out of Larry's arms and close to his breast. Above her head he looked straight into Larry's outraged eyes and grinned.

"Afraid that's it, old man," he said cheerfully.

Larry's handsome face was dark with rage.

"A fine friend you turned out to be," he snarled, "waiting until my back was turned and then making a play for my girl."

"It wasn't quite like that, Larry," said Troy quietly. "You ran out on her, remember? You abandoned her. You didn't even realize you wanted her until you discovered that I did! I was pretty dumb, too! But now I do know, and I'm afraid you're out of luck."

"Oh, I wouldn't say that!" Ellen drawled insolently, her eyes on Larry very warm. "I'd say he was *in* luck, since he doesn't really want to marry anybody. Do you, Larry darling?"

"You keep out of this," snapped Larry sharply. "You're to blame for the whole thing. If you'd gone ahead and married Troy, Gail would have married me."

"I wouldn't, Larry, truly I wouldn't," Gail told him earnestly. "I didn't say I would. I only said I'd think about it."

Larry turned on her violently, his eyes blazing.

"I suppose this is your cute little way of getting even with me because I ran out on you," he accused her.

"It isn't, Larry, truly it isn't," she protested. "The last thing in the world I ever dared to hope for was that Troy could possibly fall in love with me. Ellen is beautiful, and they'd known each other so long, and I was just a stray kitten he and Donna had befriended."

Troy said sharply, his arm tightening about her, "Stop running yourself down, sweetheart! You're ten thousand times more beautiful than Ellen could ever hope to be."

"Now wait a minute," snapped Ellen hotly.

"No, *you* wait a minute," said Troy. "Gail is kind and sweet and good and unselfish. And she's prettier than you are! But if she was as homely as unmitigated sin, she'd still be the one girl in the world I'd want to marry."

"Hear, hear!" murmured Donna sweetly, clinging to Bob, smiling at the scene before her, her eyes brilliant with sardonic amusement as she watched Larry's irate face.

"Well, that's just dandy, then," sneered Ellen, and tucked her hand through Larry's arm. "Come on, Larry; let's get out of here. There's a new floor show at the Fontainebleau I'd like to see, and we've just time if we hurry."

Larry glared down at her and released his arm, his eyes wary.

"What have you got in mind?" he demanded suspiciously.

Ellen laughed, a small, silvery tinkle of quite honest amusement.

"Oh, don't be frightened, Larry. I'm not going to try to marry you—or anybody else! Marriage is a trap, and I have no intention of letting it snap on me. There are too many places to go, too many exciting things to do. And I'm a firm believer in the maxim: 'He who travels alone travels fastest!' " she assured him gaily.

The others watched the flicker of wariness that traveled over Larry's face before he turned and looked at Gail and then at Troy.

"You understand, Troy, that after this I shall engage a new manager for my property down here?" he said sourly.

"I hope you will, Larry," Troy answered sincerely. "I have about all I can do to look after my own."

Larry's glance swung about the room, resting briefly on Donna's face and on Bob's. Then he turned to the waiting Ellen and said curtly, "Let's get out of this."

"Oh, by all means, let's," Ellen cooed sweetly. As she turned to go, she said over her shoulder, "I'll keep in touch with you, Bob, so you'll know where to send my checks."

"I feel sure you will," said Bob pleasantly, but there was a note in his voice that made her look sharply at him before she turned and swept out of the room behind Larry.

No one spoke until the sound of the car, spattering shells as it plowed out of the drive and into the highway, had died away.

It was Donna who broke the silence, and she did it by smiling tenderly at Troy. "Congratulations, darling."

Troy tightened his arm about Gail and drew her close.

"Thanks, Donna. I *am* to be congratulated now that Gail is mine."

"I don't mean congratulations because you've been lucky enough to snag Gail," Donna said cheerfully. "I congratulate you on losing Ellen. I never liked that girl. I never trusted her! But I'll have to admit I didn't think a few dollars could make so much difference in a girl."

"Well, to Ellen it wasn't just a few dollars, honey," Bob pointed out thoughtfully. "It was more money than she'd ever dreamed of, and I suppose it sort of knocked her off base."

Donna looked up at him severely.

"Now, don't you go turning noble on me," she ordered. "If there's one thing I could never stand, it's a noble husband who sees good in everything and everybody."

Bob gave a deep laugh and drew her to him.

"Then you'll be perfectly safe with me, honey," he told her. "Not even my best friend, or my worst enemy, could ever accuse me of being noble! I hope you will put up with me, though."

"It will be a pleasure," Donna assured him. "And now let's go have a look at the babes. I've a hunch Troy and Gail could endure a small smidgin of privacy about now."

"How subtle of you," mocked Troy. And Donna laughed and blew him a kiss as she and Bob left the room.

Gail was standing a little away from Troy and could not quite bring her eyes up to meet his. Troy watched her, joying in the look of her as she stood there, trembling slightly, her hands tightly locked together.

"Darling sweet," he said at last very softly.

Finally she met his eyes and asked, her soft voice shaking, "When did it happen, Troy?"

"I don't know, sweet. It sort of—well, I guess it

sneaked up on me," he admitted frankly. "At first I just grew accustomed to finding you here every night when I came home, tired out and beat! Then gradually, I began looking forward to that first glimpse of you. I think I really *knew* for the first time the night you waited up for me and I found you asleep in the living room, looking about Cissy's age! I knew that Ellen was free, that she was counting on me. I was too involved to tell you I loved you; and it wasn't a very happy thought, either."

"That was the night it really dawned on me, too," said Gail huskily. "I wouldn't admit it, even to myself, because there was Larry as well as Ellen. But when she told me she was going to make you sell out down here and go to New York to live—"

"She told you that? And you didn't warn me?"

"Oh Troy, no, of course not!" she responded. "I couldn't betray her confidence."

"Not even to spare me from her machinations?"

"That was when she told me I loved you," she answered shakily. "And she said that if I told you what she was planning, she'd tell you I'd lied because I wanted you for myself. I did, too, Troy. So you see, I couldn't tell you."

"Because you were afraid I'd think you and Ellen had been having a cat fight?" His tone, as his arms drew her close, was teasing. "Honey, don't you know that no one could ever make me believe you'd lie? You're incapable of a lie or of a dirty trick against anything or anybody. You're the most transparently honest creature I've ever known. And I love you very much."

His kiss set her heart to beating so hard that she felt it sounded like bongo drums. After a long, long moment she sighed deeply and looked up at him, her eyes dewy, her soft mouth tremulous.

"I can't believe it's really happening," she breathed. "It's too wonderful to be true."

"It's too wonderful, sweetheart, not to be true!" he told her, and once more his mouth claimed her own. And all the world was Paradise in which they two dwelt alone, because there was no need for anyone else in that lovely land.